P9-ARV-865

CHILDREN OF HEROES

Children of Heroes

Lyonel Trouillot

Translated by Linda Coverdale

University of Nebraska Press | Lincoln and London

Publication of this book was assisted by a grant from
the National Endowment for the Arts.

NATIONAL
ENDOWMENT
FOR THE ARTS

"A Great Nation Deserves Great Art"
This work, published as part of the program of aid for
publication, received support from the French Ministry of Foreign Affairs and the Cultural Service of the
French Embassy in the United States.
Cet ouvrage publié dans le cadre du programme d'aide
à la publication bénéficie du soutien du Ministère
des Affaires Etrangères et du Service Culturel de
l'Ambassade de France représenté aux Etats-Unis.

Library of Congress Cataloging-in-Publication Data
Trouillot, Lyonel.
[Enfants des héros. English]
Children of heroes / Lyonel Trouillot;
translated by Linda Coverdale.
p. cm.
ISBN 978-0-8032-4450-4 (cloth : alk. paper)
ISBN 978-0-8032-9459-2 (pbk. : alk. paper)
I. Coverdale, Linda. II. Title.
PQ3949.2.T76E6413 2008
831'.914—dc22
2007023718
Set in Adobe Caslon and Scala Sans.
Designed by Ashley Muehlbauer.

To Régis, François, Claudine,
Benjamin, Maurice, and Christine
zanmi pre
zanmi lwen
friends
near and far

"What do you know about this business?"
the King said to Alice.

"Nothing," said Alice.

"Nothing *whatever*?" persisted the King.

"Nothing whatever," said Alice.

—Lewis Carroll
Alice's Adventures in Wonderland

CHILDREN OF HEROES

It must have been noon when we began to run. We could have put up with the smell for a lot longer, but when Mariéla saw the mailman coming, a guy who never failed to have a drink with Corazón and reminisce about the legendary greats of boxing, she dumped our savings out of their jar and, warning me not to lose them, slipped the coins into my pocket, then told me to run without stopping until I was out of the slum. If we became separated along the way, she would wait for me in front of old Moses's furniture factory. She led me over to the bed where Joséphine was still sleeping. We looked one last time at that face battered by blows and the passing years. You could see the bones beneath the flesh, and those very bones seemed to be sagging, as if the whole body had cried uncle. With the passing years, she had become a transparent thing. At the last, when Corazón struck her, the blows went right through her. In that image where there had once been a woman, now only a blank remained. Asleep, she seemed even more dead than Corazón, who lay in the middle of the room, his skull split open, his body partly hidden by the chest of drawers and the chairs knocked over when he fell. All the furniture in the house had toppled onto him. The chest. The chairs. The stove and the aluminum plates. The low table where he put his feet while listening to soccer matches on the transistor radio Mam Yvonne gave us, back when she was working in the laundry of that hospital in the Bronx she described to us in her letters as sometimes a paradise and sometimes sheer hell. The kerosene lamp we used when money was tight. The pot of plastic flowers and the big stone ashtray Joséphine had bought as ornamental touches. The four little pink glasses with hearts on them. The décor and all the trimmings. Everything—or almost everything—in the house had been broken over Corazón's big body. The blue of his overalls disappeared in places beneath the debris of incongruous objects. He had lost one of his sneakers and I could see the sole of his foot, as rough as lizard skin. I preferred to look at his foot. Every time my eyes landed on his face, I felt the prickling that comes before tears, and I tried to reassure myself by behaving like Mariéla. She is the strongest, the most honest with herself. The most alone, perhaps. While we stayed in that room, she never showed one sign of weakness. She sat down in the middle of the mess, just long enough to come to a decision. Then, in a burst of energy, she stuffed our skimpy belongings into the big canvas bag where Joséphine tucked away our dirty laundry. I realized that we were going to go. Quite far away from Joséphine, who slept on in the bed where she could finally stretch out at her ease, without having to huddle up real small, hugging the wall to leave more space for Corazón's huge body. The trouble is, Joséphine has never been willing to sleep alone. As long as I've known her, she has always needed a man in her bed. A husband or a son. Her favorite is Corazón. Was. He's dead. And I won't be around anymore to replace him, now that the future belongs to the authorities. She truly loved him, Corazón. When he came home later than usual, she'd wait for him before she drew the curtain and went to bed. When he was out all night, she sat up in the chair, her mouth full of prayers. Whenever he stayed away for some time, I was his replacement. Joséphine would call me to come get into the bed. She'd hug me close for a while and fall into an uneasy sleep toward dawn, still murmuring complaints and prayers. If you begin at the end, then we are the chief culprits. No one has the right to take life away. But while we never meant to kill it, that life was turning out badly every single day. Whether he really did ever climb into the ring or whether he was just lying to us, Corazón hit every-thing that moved, except for Mariéla. So he might have expected that someday someone would hit back. And Joséphine, although you couldn't ever accuse her of loving hatred or violence, is not completely inno-cent. You might think she lives on nothing because she never asks for anything. The truth is, she rarely uses words to say things. Her expectations take a side-ways approach. She has hardly any voice and never shouts "I want," or "I mean," or "I demand." She never raises her voice, but in her eyes there's a whole vocab-ulary. To get something, her face freezes and grows pitiful. Her face is a lament that weeps over its hopes in a roundabout way. She also invents stories that often have a hidden meaning. For example, she tells how when I was little I used to run away from the clatter of rainstorms on the sheet-metal roofs. How I'd hide in the latrines shared by the small houses of the neighborhood. She believes that story cross-her-heart and tells it to anyone who'll listen. At that time, Corazón wasn't sleeping in the house. He wouldn't accept the idea of this second child. Joséphine, according to her, used to pry me from my hidey-hole, rub my limbs briskly, and keep me in her bed for the night. I don't remember escaping to the latrines, and I've always loved the sound of rain. Especially after Mariéla taught me how to change the water into music by cupping my palms over my ears. During every downpour, I'd compose songs for myself, merry little melodies. That's what I remember. Me being so scared, Joséphine invented that to express a wish: that I would fill in for Corazón in her bed whenever he spent the night drinking in one of those crummy dives where the rum's too cheap to match the label on its bottle. Joséphine, my mother, has always lived in fear that someone else would swipe her spot in her men's hearts. She wanted me to remain her frail child my whole life long. Joséphine, she's unhappy, she has no guarantee that she'll always be needed. That no other woman will ever come along to replace her. She has always been jealous of Mariéla, who asks nothing of anyone. Joséphine's failing was to worry, to believe that one day Corazón and I would both take off and leave her flat. Corazón liked to frighten her and would run away every now and then. He'd come back after each fake departure, though, and Joséphine, reassured, would give thanks for that godsend. And yet that blessing may perhaps have worked more like a curse. Each time he returned, he hated her a bit more, and beat her a bit more to make up for lost time. Me, I never thought about going away. Except for just long enough to come back, my arms full of little pink glasses decorated with hearts and my pockets stuffed with gourdes[1] and sourballs, since Joséphine never allowed herself any whims or treats save for the tons of sticky candies she gorged on every Sunday afternoon. During the week she lived on prayers and watching others eat. It was only on Sunday that she turned greedy. I would never have left, except to go get her candies. And drinking glasses just like the ones she bought from a hardware stall at the Salomon market. I'm sure she likes them better than all the lovely luxury items in the whole wide world. Joséphine, she's had a hard life, she's just suffering itself. I didn't want to abandon her. Still, she shouldn't have invented that story about the latrines. It made me feel smaller every time she trotted out that tale for Mam Yvonne or the neighbor ladies. Especially since, really, I never needed any excuse to love her. She comes right after Mariéla. And in life as in school, second place isn't so bad. Mariéla, she's in first place: I see her from inside, as if we were walking in step. To the point that sometimes I forget that we're two people, after all. Whereas Joséphine I've always loved from a certain distance. Now that I'll never see her again, because after what we've done we can't live together anymore, the distance will grow bigger without changing my feelings. You can love someone from very far away. The way it is in history lessons, which teach about the destiny of navigators who look back on their countries from afar, still feeling affection for that tiny image. Distance, that's something we didn't know how to talk about, Mariéla and I, the day Corazón died. What's far away exists without any outlines. You can't imagine its shape. All you know is, the space isn't defined. It floats a little, like a boat. It's a territory like the night, it needs time to become natural. At the moment we left, when the mailman's footsteps were approaching, Mariéla couldn't manage to explain it to me. The words weren't coming to her. Although she usually didn't have any trouble finding the right words. She has a gift for saying things, but "far away," where we had to go, she just couldn't describe it precisely. The only image that came to me was that we'd be abandoning the slum to live the rest of our lives in a kind of wasteland. I was careful not to walk on the broken glass and crockery or bump into Corazón's long legs, which divided the room almost perfectly in half. His body was still big, too big for a small one-room house with a woman and two children always getting in his way. Only his face had shrunk. He'd fallen on his side and was showing his bad profile. He had chosen, for his death mask, that fake look of a sad child he always wore after some creditor had been by. Before she took the plane to the United States, Mam Yvonne, who knew religion without being devout like Joséphine, often used to tell us that the power of the Evil One lies in guile. And that God's weapon is compassion.

Corazón must have taken after both of them. I realized this on the day he died. Joséphine experienced both those sides of him every day. Why else would she protect her face whenever he approached her with a bottle in his hand? And why did she speak to him at other times as if in supplication? Begging for his presence like a blessing! He was both her demon and her Good Lord. Even in death, he hadn't changed: Corazón was many men, all of them quite different. He could have written the book on schemes to get drunk whenever he liked and never pay his debts. He could also waver like a reluctant convalescent hesitating between the cure and a relapse. He took the worst of life and talked only about the best. That was my father: a brute who could be as gentle as a sheep. Before leaving for the United States, Mam Yvonne often used to visit us to speak heart-to-heart with Joséphine and shower her with advice. As soon as people start living better than you do, that sort of makes them an authority. Mariéla didn't much appreciate Mam Yvonne's way of lecturing us. Mariéla doesn't like wisdom. Mam Yvonne really needed to say those words to us. She felt a touch guilty about Corazón's behavior and meant to pass on to her daughter-in-law her expertise as a capable woman. Men, they're all pigs. A smart woman uses men and doesn't let them push her around. All of them, without exception: pigs, and nothing more. My son's just like the rest of them. And Joséphine, who had a loving heart right out of the movies, would start defending Corazón. Mam Yvonne admitted that he wasn't bad through and through. But watch out. When he was little, I caught him several times putting burning cigarette butts in the ear of the milkman's donkey or ripping the pages from a schoolbook to avoid doing his homework. He fought frantically to escape the spankings he'd earned. He would put on the face of an angel and soon you'd forgive him. Mam Yvonne warned Joséphine: even as a child, he was always capable of doing terrible things. And now Corazón would lose his temper, start choking, sucking up all the air in the room, and we'd all feel the tension mount. Before the impassive Mam Yvonne, Corazón would be fuming, almost shouting, but he never dared challenge her openly. Yes, you used to do that, she would insist. Then you'd go bragging to your friends, whose mothers would tell me about it. Mam Yvonne would search her memory for years, dates, witnesses, while Corazón gave way, reduced to telling us that his mother had made up that business about the cigarette butts in the donkey's ears just to make us think badly of him and to cause trouble in his own home. Joséphine already doesn't respect me, so if you start sticking your nose in . . . I have to admit that I agreed with him. Mothers, they always come up with stuff that doesn't exactly reflect reality, it's more like the idea they have of their sons. Take Joséphine and those latrines. A mother, she's fine. Except when she sets about telling the story of your life. The more the son grows up, committing his own fresh follies, the more the mother clings to the follies of the past. When there aren't enough, she invents them. On that point, Joséphine was like Mam Yvonne, constantly claiming the right to meddle by deciding what my favorite meal was, or putting her seal on my childhood memories. With a mother, things get complicated if she decides to know you better than you know yourself. Mam Yvonne was describing her son the way she'd wanted him to be, while he put on his lost-child face and seemed about to burst the seams of his overalls, his muscles swelling with vexation. And knowing that soon Mam Yvonne would no longer be there to protect us from the storm she had a talent for stirring up, Joséphine would ask Mariéla and me to go get some Barbancourt rum on credit at old man Eliphète's variety store. Softly she'd remind us to make sure Eliphète put it on her tab, since Corazón had long since exhausted his credit in every business in the neighborhood. We'd bring back the rum. At the sight of the bottle, Corazón would simmer down, relax his muscles, and trot out his favorite saying: Life holds only bad surprises, and the last one will be death. When it comes, I won't put up a fuss. Well, death came. Despite what people say, we didn't go out looking for it. It wasn't cooked up in advance. Violence attracts more violence, and Mariéla lifted up that wrench as if she had become a kind of robot handpicked by horror, or Providence. The teacher had explained to us that despite what historians say (they only ever know the outside of events), it wasn't the lunatic Défilée who gathered up the remains of Emperor Dessalines the evening of his assassination, but a brave spirit passing across the bridge who took over the old madwoman's body.[2] History, she told us, hides a wealth of mysteries and as many surprises. No one knows beforehand who among us will become a hero or a monster. As for Corazón, although there was nothing historic about his death, he was definitely and forever fresh out of surprises. He still lay there, and Mariéla didn't spare him even a single glance. Me, I would have liked to speak with him one last time. To talk. Present our case. Argue with his corpse. Find words that would be halfway between a "Sorry" and "Goodbye." Explain to him. Lecture him. But Mariéla would not have tolerated such a compromise. The mailman's footsteps were drawing closer, leaving us little time. It must have been noon. I could hear the little kids shouting over at the elementary school. Their shrill tumult drowned out the ringing of the bell announcing the end of classes. I recognized the voices of my friends in the uproar: Roland, Ambroise, and all the others. Marcel. And especially Stammering Jhonny, but his voice you can't hear because he needs at least an hour to say the slightest thing. So, he prefers to keep quiet. Jhonny is my best friend. If Corazón hadn't drunk up Mam Yvonne's last check, I would have been out yelling with them, yanking the back hem of the proctor's jacket, and maybe Mariéla wouldn't have done what she did. Or she would have done it all by herself. In a way, you might say that it was a blessing in disguise, that habit Corazón had fallen into, of spending my school fee money in the bar. Spending that money, that's one thing I've forgiven him. School I never liked. And I was always a slow learner. Unlike Mariéla. She understands everything right away. My essays, she used to write them for me in no time, while it took me forever to compose the first line. The teacher used to emphasize the importance of an outline, the sequence of ideas, the structure of paragraphs. "You went on a picnic with your parents: tell us about it. Describe a sunset. Draw up the portrait of your favorite animal." I'd try to plan an outline. But I couldn't decide on the right trees and animals to invent. Should I begin the description with the roots or the fur or the tail, the moral or the physical portrait, the frame or the color? Mariéla would take the pencil from my hand. In the time it took me to jump a hedge, or pull on a rope, or lob some dumb I-dare-you at Marcel or Stammering Jhonny, or stroll around the neighborhood spying on the pretty girls who went to the Baptist church without obeying the commandments, she'd whipped me up a landscape all my own, a sea just right for a voyage, a dog, a cat, a big house with real windows and a door set straight on its hinges. She'd even written me some wonderful parents: a father who didn't beat me and a mother with a gift for smiles. At first the teacher had ranked me among the poorest pupils. As Mariéla kept writing for me, my compositions improved along with my grades until I was even held up as an example. Until the day the teacher told Joséphine that I was a born writer. And Joséphine, while she wasn't a blabbermouth, once she'd drawn the curtain and shut herself in with Corazón at the back of the room, after begging us to go play outside so we wouldn't hear her sighs, well, she couldn't keep anything secret from him. Corazón, he soon figured out that Mariéla was the author. He said it was a father's place to keep an eye on his son's work and that he would go to the school to talk with the teacher. Joséphine gave him the money. When I was sent home because my fees were late, she didn't dare ask Corazón about it for fear he'd fly into a rage and beat the hell out of us both. About school, though, it's not so serious. It's really something I never regretted. Mariéla stopped going after she got her certificate. And I mean, school is no party. Fortunately, it's not because of this that Mariéla did what she did. That we did what we did. Together. Corazón's death, I can't say that I'm proud of it. It wasn't worked out ahead of time. You shouldn't claim credit for actions unless you planned them. And it wasn't a success, either, like a discovery you make or when you create something new. We fell into it, Corazón's death. It's a trap life had set for us a long time before. An event that will live on in the annals of the city. Given that neither time nor other people will allow us to forget it. Don't ever think I'm proud of it. Ever since that day, though, Mariéla and I, we're like a community. Even if they separate us, we'll always be together. A team. I'm the one who held Corazón's feet to make him slip. Before that, Mariéla had had to do her best for the both of us. When I was really little, she used to take care of me when Joséphine was lost in her prayers. When I was sick with malaria, it was Mariéla who gave me my medicine, checking the instructions to figure out the dosage. If I had the power, there are times when I'd like to bring him back to life, Corazón. Especially at night. He isn't mean when he's asleep. No, I'm not proud of what we did. But, on the other hand, it's good that she didn't have to do it alone. Mariéla is too all alone. This time, at least she'll be able to say: My little brother helped me.

Hearing the mailman's footsteps, Mariéla grabbed the bag she'd filled with our clothes and pushed me toward the door. Outside, the first thing that struck me was the heat of the sun. Mariéla and I, we prefer the moon. On moonlit nights, shadows are softer than modeling clay, and we used to draw shapes with them. The noonday sun casts a shadow so hard that it follows close on your heels, as if everyone had a personal policeman to drag along underfoot. We always took shelter when the sun beat down too harshly. At school, there was the great oak in the middle of the recreation yard. Mariéla had also shown me other shady places for escaping the sunshine. Sometimes we hid behind the long curtains of sheets hung up by washerwomen. Or we sought out the dampness of the unfinished little houses at the far end of the slum. Out where stubborn folks had begun to build despite warnings from the city inspectors and then reluctantly had to stop work after all, because you cannot lay foundations in a swamp. The two of us had always had our haunts, spots where we could outwit the sun. For the first time, we had to brave the glare without the promise of relief, trying courageously to outrun it, racing for a long time toward the night. After Corazón's death, the first thing I saw was the sun. The second thing, that was the mailman's belly. I ran right into it. He let the whole neighborhood's mail tumble into the stagnant water between our place and the Jean-Baptiste family's house next door. The letters began to spread out into the muddy water and float like sailboats. The neighbors might have forgiven us for just Corazón. Basically, aside from us, no one liked him. He'd wheedled money from even the poorest of the poor, and since the women liked his looks, all the men loathed him without daring to tell him so, because of his biceps. Our real crime was to have knocked the mail into the muck. No one in the world likes having their hopes flung into a puddle. People were going to shred us. There was surely a letter from Mam Yvonne swimming somewhere in there. Corazón could sense them coming and would get the little table ready to welcome the mailman, who loved to chat with him about boxing. One bottle, two glasses. Corazón had a mongrel's flair for sniffing out the arrival of Mam Yvonne's letters and arranged to intercept them so he could spend the money himself. On those days, Corazón, who no longer allowed Joséphine to leave the house, encouraged her instead to go out, reminding her of this or that promise to visit an old friend. He'd set the glasses on the table, roll up his sleeves to admire his biceps, and wait for the mailman. He was rarely off in his calculations, and then only by a day or two. Except for those six months when we went without any news, which was how long it took Mam Yvonne to get the backlog of her Social Security checks from the state of Florida. Floating among the letters was one from Mam Yvonne with a number to be presented at the window of the foreign exchange office and precise instructions as to the usage of the sum in question. But now Corazón would not be there to intercept it. And anyway, the mail for the whole slum was soaking in the puddle between our house and the Jean-Baptiste place. The mailman had gotten to his feet and was shouting at us to come back. We were long gone when he decided to enter our house to get help from someone with authority. We had already run down half the main alley, passed the entrance to the elementary school, and were climbing over the dilapidated little wall around the property of the pastor of the Baptist church to take the shortcut that came out in front of the furniture factory. Grown-ups avoid that path, especially those with jobs, because they risk stepping on broken glass or cow-pats: the smell of dung is unmistakable, and grown-ups don't always like people to know where they've been. For us, though, it's so simple to jump over the low wall. And since no boss preaches to us on payday about the need for cleanliness, we prefer the shortcut to the adults' long ways around. At the end of the path, only a hop, skip, and a jump from the asphalt where the big city began, Fat Mayard tried to stop us, just for fun. Actually, I didn't interest him. I don't interest many people. To them— aside from Stammering Jhonny, Marcel, and a few others—I'm Mariéla's brother. Fat Mayard felt honor bound to feel up girls' breasts, and he often lay in wait for Mariéla. She had let him do it once, probably because it was a new experience. Mariéla likes trying new things. And he, foolishly convinced he'd acquired some rights, had gone all around the slum crowing victory to make guys jealous. On the day of Corazón's death, he tried to grab her and hold her close. At first it was only a game. When he heard the uproar of the neighborhood shouting our names, he realized something serious had happened. Like everyone who dreams of being in the spotlight, he tried to join in, by grabbing Mariéla for real. And she dodged him. Exactly like Corazón when he worked out at daybreak while the neighborhood still slept, except for the women on their way home from the bakery with bread to sell. That threw Fat Mayard for a loop, but he wouldn't give up. An unarmed girl was supposed to be easy prey. He pounced again. And Mariéla treated him to the shock of his life. She popped him one right in the breadbasket. Just the way Corazón shadow-boxed with the morning breeze to keep in shape. In a last reflex of pride, Fat Mayard took the precaution of glancing around. No one was watching. Relieved to have no witnesses, he dropped to his knees, eyes glazed, breathless, gagging as if giving up the ghost. We didn't have time to scold him, to tell him he was going to live and get himself clobbered plenty more times. Flesh isn't as weak as people think. Mariéla and I know that death doesn't kill with a single punch, it's the accumulation of damage that wears the body down from inside, till only the skin is left. Those last weeks, Corazón hit Joséphine almost every day. She didn't even bleed anymore, didn't cry, didn't react in any way. But her battered skin kept breathing. Death hadn't yet risen to the surface. Blows take a long time to kill. Fat Mayard could wait. Mariéla burst out laughing at his look of despair. Some people come into this world with the gift of tears. Mariéla's natural-born talent is laughter. She'd found that out all by herself, no help needed. I don't know if there are places where laughing is taught, but around here you just pick it up on your own. And sometimes life goes by so fast or stays in one spot so long that somehow you run out of time or energy and never get around to learning. Me, for example, I don't like to laugh. In elementary school they teach you the ABCs. The different churches of God teach the fear of the Lord. For wisdom and rules to live by, we take inspiration from proverbs. In our neighborhood, when things go wrong, life leans on proverbs. Everyone has a supply of them. Even the poorest souls. And they're the only possession we share without waiting to be asked. Those times when we have nothing to say to one another, we toss out a proverb at random, and that can start up who knows what conversation. We've got tons of proverbs to fill empty spaces and provide commentary for any occasion. Even those unexpected once-in-a-lifetime events. When the rainy season lasted so long that the water topped the highest roofs of the houses clinging down in the ravines, people were racking their brains to come up with a saying that would explain the deluge. The oldsters invent a proverb every time misfortune trips life up. And children collect them to grow in wisdom. Mariéla's laughter isn't some local custom, it's a personal conquest. Mariéla is her very own creation. Her tears, her ideas, her peals of laughter. And now her destiny. If you can call the trackless life ahead of us a destiny. She was still laughing when we reached a real street. With a name. And cars. A different territory under different rules. In our neighborhood, aside from those who work and always slog home exhausted, we have lots of spare time. So people are available. Our pursuers weren't about to give up the chase, but it would be hard for them to find us in the crowd. We'd become a girl and boy among others. Anonymous in the real city. The one on the map. Once we'd reached the outskirts of the city, we slowed down. I was coughing. Pedestrians were turning around and seemed to study me with a suspicious eye. I can't help coughing after the slightest effort. In the slum, my cough is no big deal. Everybody knows it's part of my nature, a constitutional defect, and no one pays any attention. But strangers always seem a little startled by it. Our headlong run had worn me out, so Mariéla suggested we go on to the Champ-de-Mars, to rest there on a bench.[3] We walked slowly and my cough calmed down. I had no idea what would happen next, but I felt fine. The anxiety came later, on the bench. And again that evening, when we had to improvise to find a place to sleep. And yet again the next day, when we went to meet Stammering Jhonny and found out the press had gotten involved. Black thoughts, they're like trees. They can take time to grow, budding in your head, and wind up taking root there. During those first hours after Corazón had died for real, after our race to escape the slum, we walked quietly around the Champ-de-Mars, where the statues of heroes look down indifferently from on high. Mariéla was carrying the sack and thinking for the two of us. We walked side by side, and I advanced calmly, as if I were hidden behind her. She has always been kind to me. She's done heaps of favors for me, a thousand little things you don't think about at the time. Big things, too. Like doing my homework or taking care of my health. Plus, since she was Corazón's favorite child, whenever I misbehaved she'd say *we*, to soften him up. If it isn't against the law, I hope we'll be able to write to each other. She and I, we were a real pair. Mariéla is more than a sister. Brother and sister, they're not words we use. In the slum we call everyone by name and we more or less love whomever we like. We can't afford to love from obligation. I had chosen Mariéla. It was already like that before. And for as long as our escape lasted—three days, two moons, and a few hours—until they spotted us on the third day on that same Champ-de-Mars, watched over by those same statues, me sitting at the bandstand, dreaming about music, and she returning from her bike ride, the two of us formed a real pair.

When we reached the Champ-de-Mars, we slowed down and looked for an empty bench. To take a rest. Every seat was taken. The only free space was the corner of a marble bench already occupied by a gentleman dressed the old way. In a three-piece suit and tie. And although he didn't say a word, we understood that he spoke a different language from ours. A library language with difficult words. He did not answer our hello. At any other time, Mariéla would have insisted, pressuring the man into politeness. The man did not see us, refusing the accidental company of such offspring from another world. Hands lying flat upon his thighs, he looked into the distance, indifferent to everything, not just our presence. But still. You're supposed to reply when spoken to. Although Mariéla was the sort to make him eat his own tie, we weren't in a position to stand up for good manners. We were rather like him, staring solitarily at our horizon line. Except that ours was behind us. Or maybe off to the side. The man was one of those lucky people who know where to look. A scholar or a man of faith. He was at peace in his world. Still keeping an eye on our strange neighbor, Mariéla asked me to dig the money out of my pocket so we could count up our fortune. Then she wanted to know if I was hungry, and I answered no. I'd been thinking, too. After what we'd done, I'd lost the right to be frail. I'd decided to be grown-up. To summon some strength. So I'd promised myself to control my cough. And not to be hungry or thirsty. Ever again. To live without anything. Without daring to feel the slightest need. Not in front of Mariéla, in any case. You're sure you're not hungry? I said no, and besides, it was true. The first day, I didn't want anything. To make things equal between us, I asked her if she wanted me to take charge of the bag. In the future. No, it's not very heavy. Mariéla never speaks with the voice of a victim. There were bloodstains on her dress. More real than the gentleman with the well-cut clothes who continued to stare straight ahead of him without moving his head or his hands, seeing only the portent of that imaginary line he had chosen to target. So I copied him. I gazed at an empty point to avoid seeing the bloodstains on the dress, and all that had happened. Sitting on that bench made me vulnerable. (Before Corazón's death, I lived on silence and would stay motionless for long periods. Now I need movement. And floods of words. Silence awakens the dead.) Corazón was already taking advantage of our stay on the bench to become a kind of ghost. He was there, before my eyes. I looked at Mariéla. Even in the heart of death, Mariéla is like life. But he was coming between us. Enormous.

Bleeding from open wounds. Working hard at dying. If you don't want to think about anything, you must take life like an athlete, run all the time, hide behind speed. Once the body is at rest, misery swarms into your head. I stared straight ahead. I looked up at the statues, and I still saw the blood. I closed my eyes to concentrate better. But it's inside your head that you see. The images come from within. That's where everything happens and then happens all over again, real fast. Corazón was dead, and he was alive. Ready to die anew. And now here in the afternoon it's morning once more. It's like a play or a movie. I close my eyes to stay in the afternoon. But the morning is stubborn. Eternal. Unstoppable. Despite all my efforts to stay where we are, Mariéla and I are walking past the garage again. We're returning from the market. A long walk for not much: a pepper and some laundry detergent. The pepper is for Corazón. So's the detergent, for his overalls. The garage isn't too far from the slum. We usually avoid that street. Corazón doesn't like to be bothered at work. And to see him is to bother him. Or not to see him: same thing. Because he doesn't go there every day. The toolbox, the tools, the overalls, all that, it's for show. He doesn't really work at the garage. He's used more like an automobile jack there. He has no claims on the machinery. Or dignity. Or words. Corazón, he's a pair of arms. But we don't know that. Mariéla, who wanted to take that street, she doesn't know that. There's an unbelievable scene going on at the garage. An end-of-the-world. One voice is raised, dominating the others. It isn't Corazón's. On the contrary: the louder that voice grows, the weaker Corazón's gets. We watch what's going on. Mariéla is very upset. On her face I can see astonishment, then disappointment. The scene is hard to describe because what we see is way more humiliating than a kid driven by fear into the shit of the public latrines. This job? The only reason you've got it is because of a promise to your father! Corazón is dying. And don't you dare have any more opinions or touch one single thing without being asked! It's as if one of the grand statues on the Place des Héros had fallen from its pedestal. Physically he's still very much alive and is lifting a section of an engine, those are the boss's orders. But he's a man without an image. And Mariéla, who has always respected him even when she disapproved of him, now realizes she's an orphan. She takes my hand and we leave. We drop the detergent we were to bring back to Joséphine. And the pepper. Mariéla stomps on the pepper and picks up the detergent. She doesn't want to go home right away. We walk. We're looking for an image, a reason to tell ourselves that it's not serious. But the walk doesn't erase the scene. We've already seen everything that's in the street. It's all ugly, all the same: the beggars, the dust, the shop signs, the drunks. And us. There's nothing that could protect us from Corazón's fall. I hear the boss's voice. Lousy good-for-nothing! And lots of adjectives for Corazón run through our minds. None of them positive. He's a man without quality who has no rights or privileges. And Mariéla says to me, He'll never hit you again. She thought of me, and I of Joséphine. Between Mariéla and Joséphine, there's no love lost. Joséphine adores being pitied and Mariéla despises weaklings. The sun's broiling our skin and we decide to go home. But we still dawdle. We need time to accept Corazón in his new version. We're hoping not to see him again right away. It's like when Jhonny's older brother had his crazy fit. I saw him. On all fours, like a dog. Wagging, like a dog, his imaginary tail. Lapping dirty water from a ditch, like a dog. When Jhonny told me that the fit had passed and that his brother thought he was human again, I waited weeks before seeing him. So as not to see the dog. It takes time to get used to the new reality of a father who gets himself told off and walked all over like a rag. Unfortunately, when we get home he's already there. He has set up the table, with the bottle and the glasses. The dead hero acts as though he were alive. He's waiting for the mailman. He can't forgive Joséphine for bustling around the house. For being there. For wearing such a sad look that you can't miss it. She's busy. And always sad. When she's not cooking, she cleans house or mends old clothing. Housework is her passion. It's kind of amazing. If you look around, you won't find that many objects to put away. We don't live in a big house, and when she insists on straightening up the place, moving things around and dusting the glasses, everyone feels uncomfortable. Especially Corazón, who has no more room to stretch out his legs. He usually chases her out when he's expecting the mailman. They're alone in the house, and he's starting to get cross. That part, I don't see that, it's something I imagine. He can't bear Joséphine looking at him even though she's as meek as can be. But he knows perfectly well that he's a worthless man, and he believes she knows that too. Even though she has always found reasons to admire him. She's the only one who can forgive him. Even Mam Yvonne has lost all hope. She went away to wait until he can't make decisions for us anymore. So that she can salvage us. Mam Yvonne is figuring that we'll find a way to replace him. She gives us presents and is secretly preparing our departure for abroad. Even his mother has abandoned Corazón. His only absolution is Joséphine. Mariéla loved him when she thought he was her equal. They communicated over our heads. Now Mariéla is all alone. Only she has the strength to face up, to decide. She's ready to pay the price. While he lay low like a lizard in front of his boss, to save a lie. You do what I tell you, or you get out. And don't come sniveling back around here. Corazón, he gave in, so he could keep his overalls. And now he wants to play the big guy. Joséphine's presence enrages him. When we walk in, he's hitting her. With each blow he lands, he's trying to hide the truth. He doesn't care that we're there. He has no idea that we saw him die not an hour before. He hits her. To re-create the image he lost. But he's not our champion anymore. Nothing but some poor jerk and our father. We arrive just when his huge fist lands in Joséphine's face and destroys it, propelling her to the back of the room, toward the bed. And he's not finished. He goes after her, defending his imaginary titles. He keeps his guard up, he's Joe Louis again: Joe hoists up Joséphine, who's already knocked out from the first blows. Joe is boxing. And the old skin bag is taking a beating. For Mam Yvonne, whom he never dared to challenge. For the garage owner, who treats him like less than zero. For El Negro, the Dominican boxer against whom he lasted only a single round that one time he ever stepped into a real ring. For the referee, who stopped the fight too early, before I got my second wind. That ref, he fucked up my whole life. And suddenly, he's punching her for Mariéla, who's ordering him to stop. Up yours! Here, I'm the boss! He pummels his punching bag exultantly. But he's been dead ever since the incident at the garage. He's been dead ever since we heard him stammer helplessly. That's why Mariéla goes rummaging through the box where he keeps his tools. She hefts the wrenches, selects the heaviest one. Corazón, basking in his glory, still thinks he holds his audience in the palm of his hand. Mariéla goes up to him, then up on tiptoe to take better aim at his skull, and sweeps her arms in an arc to bring that wrench down in both hands as hard as she can. He's astonished to be attacked by an adversary he hasn't picked out himself. He thinks it's not fair, given that she's the one he loves the most. He moves toward her, perhaps to demand an explanation. He wants to understand. But Mariéla doesn't feel like having a conversation. She strikes him a second time. Head on. Right on the forehead. I hear the sound the bone makes. Now he's furious. He advances in spite of the blows, fist raised, to defend himself. That's when I intervene. I don't want him to touch Mariéla. Joséphine, she's a consenting adult. The only thing you can do for her is help her suffer, and that's all she asks. If anyone told her to leave she'd simply say mind your own business. But Mariéla, she was born to have wings. I crawl toward Corazón. I'm not afraid of him anymore. I'm only afraid of Joséphine, who will accuse Mariéla. I'm afraid because I love Joséphine and hope she will forgive us. Anyway, I crawl toward Corazón. I cling to his feet. The only thing I want is to hold him back. I forbid him to touch her. I try to bite him. My teeth aren't strong enough to get through his mechanic's overalls. He drags me along as he closes in on Mariéla. What's happening is between them; what I'm doing doesn't count. He stopped taking me seriously the day he realized that I had no talent for boxing. He moves forward as if I didn't exist. But because he's already staggering and I tighten my grip, he ends up falling. Mariéla has stopped hitting him. It's the first time I watch someone die, but I know that he's dead. I can't tell if it's the blow or the fall that killed him. Joséphine is sleeping, curled up on the bed. Her husband is lying on the floor, and the blood pools like the rain that sometimes leaks through the roof. At the time, I don't pay attention to a whole bunch of details. I didn't see the blood spurt onto Mariéla's dress. It's only on this bench in the Champ-de-Mars, next to this apathetic gentleman, that I notice the blood on the dress and realize the permanent nature of what has happened. Violence, that's something we've always lived with: in our neighborhood, the strongest beat up the weakest, and life goes on. This act went beyond anything that came before. Everything we'd ever been or said simply didn't matter anymore. Corazón's death would begin us: Joséphine, Mariéla, and me. I understood that when I saw the blood on the dress. I told myself that it was important for Joséphine not to grow old with the idea that it was a real crime. Mariéla and I, in all our predictions, had never had anything but happy endings. No child in the neighborhood is rich enough to believe in Father Christmas, but sometimes I let myself think that I could stand in for him. Then I would buy a garage for Corazón, and hundreds of glasses and loads of hard candies for Joséphine. Clothes, too, because the mother of Father Christmas deserves a wardrobe, after all. I thought about that on our bench. I saw that Mariéla was shaking, that doubts or worries had made her fragile, and I looked away, toward the gentleman. I felt tears on my cheeks and said, It's nothing, it's my cough. Mariéla pretended not to notice that I was crying.

W e sat on the bench for about an hour. The sun was sinking in the sky. The apathetic gentleman hadn't turned toward us even once. He seemed to be staring steadily at a single spot, and nothing—not the noise of the traffic, or us, his close neighbors, or the uniformed parade of officials streaming from the Palais des Ministères—could distract him. Judging from his suit and his unwavering concentration on that real or imagined spot, I had guessed that he was a gentleman who read books. The only time Joséphine had dared to ask Corazón about the school money he had drunk up glass by glass, he'd laughed, exclaiming that reading books was only good for creating loonies who think the moon is made of green cheese and don't know the simplest things, like how to drive a nail or take proper care of their families. Sometimes Corazón talked like a father. He'd give Joséphine the word "family" as a gift. It was an idea she truly cherished. Whenever he said that word, Joséphine's eyes brightened in delight. He'd watch her to gauge the impression he was making. And both of them were happy. "A man can't feed his family on books." To make us understand what a man's life is like, he'd tell us about Joe Louis. Joe Louis was his idol. He knew all his fights. Rather, he didn't know them, having only the ability to imagine them. The way he could imagine lots of things that were completely false, and take them for the truth. When he was having a drink with the mailman, he often used to act out the former champion's combinations. If he had enough money to pay off some of his debts, he'd go meet with the neighborhood tough guys and replay a few of the champ's fights for them. Joe Louis was the best. There've been some great technicians, but Joe's edge was his courage. He'd take his stand in the middle of the ring and wait for his opponent. Sometimes he'd get a faceful, but there wasn't anything complicated about it—whoever hit hardest and landed the most punches wound up the winner. To me, that's a man, someone life hasn't taught to retreat. The indifferent gentleman with the blank stare and the delicate wrists who was sharing our bench doesn't fit into Corazón's category of honorable men, and I can't imagine him making a living with his hands. With no more of a goodbye than he'd said hello, he stood up, as fluid as a phantom, slowly forded the stream of passersby, and vanished. The last employees leaving the Palais jostled one another, each trying to reach the street before the others. They looked like a people on the run from something, each one trying not to be the last to flee. Taxis were waiting for the ladies. The men set off on foot, without a backward glance. A real long time ago, when Corazón was just a kid, Mam Yvonne had worked in public service. Before her plane trip, she spoke only of the past, claiming that in her day, ladies didn't sleep with their supervisors. All this talk about the past aggravated Corazón, because the conclusion was always the same: Corazón had ruined his life with that business of going to try his luck in the Dominican Republic. Boxing, that's not a profession. You could have . . . Corazón and Joséphine agreed on one thing, at least: they both hated talking about their pasts, especially their childhoods. They could never bring themselves to say: When I was little . . . Maybe they'd had it even tougher growing up than we did, or else yesterday was just so different from today that it didn't matter anymore. I put together a past for Corazón with the little bits I had. The photos Mam Yvonne had shown us, the things she'd talked about. I could see him lighting a fire in a donkey's ear, buttering up Mam Yvonne. Quarreling with his father. Growing in strength and taking off one day for the Dominican Republic. As for Joséphine, I was sure she hadn't spent her whole life praying and getting pounded by her husband, but although I tried and tried, I could never put a smile on her little-girl face, or a ribbon in her hair. They didn't have a past to give us. Joséphine's was some information Mariéla read in the paper, when it was already too late to form a bond. Joséphine and Corazón didn't come out of anywhere. They were right there, loving or hating one another in such a mixed-up way that even they probably misunderstood their own feelings. Their silence made nonsense of the thousand and one proverbs parroted by old folks to help youngsters grow in wisdom. What good is it to repeat that tigers give birth to tigers, that pumpkins don't grow on calabash trees, like father like son, and other pretentious sayings, when you don't even know what your weepy mother's favorite colors are, when you're not even sure that the father you worship ever actually set foot in a ring, when all you know comes down to one praying and the other hitting, one crying and the other drinking? After the neighborhood people chased us down on the square and handed us over to the authorities on the third day, we were questioned by experts in this sort of thing, who attributed evil instincts and criminal intentions to us. Among our interrogators was a kindly, affable gentleman, quite nicely dressed (rather like the man on the bench), who kept harping on the suffering Corazón and Joséphine's constant quarreling must have caused us. He was disappointed to learn that my sleep wasn't cluttered with nightmares and that Mariéla hadn't grown up having nervous breakdowns. I tried to describe for him exactly how things were. He was convinced that old, unbearable traumas I had chosen to forget were wriggling deep down in my memory. Yet I wasn't hiding anything from him: I told him everything I knew about my life—and everyone else's, too. The only thing I kept to myself was the time I tried to be like Corazón. When I spent three days looking for a donkey to see what would happen if I popped a butt into its ear. Donkeys are hard to find these days. The man reminded me of Joséphine, the way she insists on deciding what's going through your own head, so I thought to ask: How's Mother? Politely, since it wasn't my place to ask questions. He replied that she was bearing up and that the Women's Action League, ladies who deal specially with ladies' problems, would help her through this difficult period. That I was asking this type of question was something he noted as a point in my favor. He was proud of me, like the quiz masters on children's radio shows when a contestant finds the right answer. "Violence in daily life instills in adolescents a chronic fear of expressing themselves." That's a sentence I remember. The man said it several times when he was talking to other people. He acted as if there had never been anyone else but Joséphine and Corazón in our lives. Actually, we'd grown tired of their fights, just as the whole neighborhood had. Back when I was in preschool, our area was still under construction. Craving entertainment, people would gather in front of our house to watch the show. Since the script never changed (there aren't a hundred thousand ways to beat your wife, after all), the public had deserted our doorway as the years went by, and no one bothered anymore to step up on a brick to peek through the window. There were churches, the lottery, and for young people, the pathetic discothèque where they serve nothing but tafia and locally brewed beer, a place that never has any lights. The owners are the only ones who complain about the thieving customers who steal their light bulbs. No one else cares. They all agree that for dancing, bodies see better in the dark. Mariéla goes there sometimes, in spite of Joséphine's tears. Mariéla invited me along last Christmas. When she feels like it, she can be very formal about things. To establish their importance. She had put on her most beautiful dress, and she was the one paying for the beer. Every male in the slum tried to get her to dance. If the guy was handsome or spoke nicely, she let herself be led off to the far end of the room. Then she'd come back to me. Sometimes, turning down an invitation, to tease me she would say, I'm dancing only with my friend here. My head was spinning—it was the first time I'd ever had a beer. All the women, that night, became so lovely. And Mariéla was the loveliest of all. I was light-headed, the way I get when my feelings overwhelm me. She looked at me tenderly and became even more beautiful. Then she took my hand to lead me out onto the floor. To dance. I hung back. I've never made the effort to learn how. When others practiced setting their steps to music on their transistor radios, I'd always thought that was a bit silly. And I was scared of myself. Was it the music or the beer? It wasn't normal that she suddenly seemed so beautiful and that I felt so different at the touch of her hand. She led me all the way to the back, to what's called Lovers' Corner. Now there was only Mariéla, and I was so happy. When I told the man, he seemed quite upset. I just wanted him to understand: our days belonged to Joséphine and Corazón. Rum for him, washing for her. And even when Corazón wasn't there, Joséphine managed to evoke his presence. She'd mention him in her prayers, tell us the secret of the dish she was fixing for him. The stove would smoke up the room, so I couldn't help coughing. Joséphine would have liked to set it up outside in an alley, someplace more or less clean. Corazón wouldn't let her. Our days belonged to them, but we knew how to save our nights. We'd stay out as late as possible, loitering around in the alleyways of the slum. Some evenings, Mariéla would vanish behind a section of wall. I'd hear her laughing, then nothing but murmurs. I suppose she'd made her choice among her admirers. On those occasions, I'd hang out with Stammering Jhonny and Marcel. Their parents didn't massacre each another as regularly as mine did, but all kids probably have their reasons for staying out until dark. So what if we all lived on top of one another—we still have our secrets to protect. You're only your true self at night. Mariéla would return with her laughter but without saying the name of her friend. She had sad evenings, too. And would come back to us disappointed. Although they're no gentlemen, Stammering Jhonny and Marcel would ask her permission to walk us home. And we'd go back through the tangled alleys of the slum. My friends would come as far as the huge puddle between our house and the Jean-Baptiste place. At home we'd find the curtain closed. Joséphine would wake up and say our bedtime prayers for us. On lucky evenings, Corazón was already home and snoring, at peace with himself. He usually came back quite late. After we did. Joséphine would be whimpering in despair at having to get through part of the night alone. She'd wait for him before drawing the curtain. We'd have to spread out our mattress and slip into our nightwear while she watched, still saying our prayers. As if it were our fault. As if she hoped for our help in bringing the missing man to his senses. Finally, Mariéla would get fed up. She'd close the curtain herself and leave Joséphine in her darkened half room with her waiting, her hopes, and her

God. Joséphine and Mariéla have never said good-night to one another. They lived without greetings. Once the curtain was drawn, Mariéla went to bed first, on her back, arms folded behind her neck. She looked at the ceiling, or beyond, toward the stars. And I looked at her. As soon as we entered the house, she became my landscape. Then I would join her. We'd discuss the day and rehearse our dreams. We always prepared them beforehand, in the dark. You can't trust sleep. Sometimes it offers you nothing, as stingy as bone-dry dirt. There are meager nights that don't attract dreams. We would get ours ready before letting sleep fool us. The next morning, we'd recount them. Corazón had to step over our mattress to go outside. His heavy tread would awaken us. Mariéla would speak first—she has more imagination than I do. The themes and characters of her dreams were always changing; in the days leading up to Corazón's death, she dreamed about a bathing suit. My dreams were mostly all alike. String and paste, colored paper and clever hands to make kites. That started when I was six, and I haven't changed. Mariéla used to tell me, You've got to change, you're old enough to dream about girls. But I still prefer kites. You've told me this one a hundred times! But there's no rule that says you have to change dreams. Jhonny and I, we used to dream about being businessmen, managing a kite factory. Real kites. Not old plastic junk with rag tails and poorly pasted frames that can't survive the snares of power lines. While I was dreaming of kites, Mariéla was traveling far away. Corazón would hear us whispering. What are you yakking about? Come and exercise instead. Exercising, that meant contemplating him. He was inviting us to watch his half-hour battle against imaginary enemies. We'd put away the mattress and go outside, where our presence boosted his morale. He shadowboxed with the wind, throwing hooks and uppercuts. That's how Mariéla learned to fight. She watched him, memorizing his movements to practice them later. From some old pieces of canvas she'd made a punching bag she hung in one of the abandoned shacks at the far end of the slum. Whenever she had a score to settle with life, or simply needed to *move* to avoid dying benumbed from living always in the same place, she'd go pound the bag. As hard as she could. One day when she was especially on edge, she threw the bag on the ground and sat astride it, still punching. That day she killed the bag. Almost. The next day, without any explanation, she hung it back in its usual place. This bag, I have to say, was sort of her Joséphine. But the people she attacked the Sunday we were caught, that was self-defense. Even though we were the guilty ones, according to the law, those people were pressing us hard, they were everywhere, as if the whole square were after us. Except for the birds and the statues. Old folks and children alike, all trying to grab us by force. When we'd already decided to go to the police station. We'd missed Joséphine's appeal on television, but Marcel and Stammering Jhonny told us that the whole neighborhood was proud of Joséphine's appearance on the screen. So naturally we wanted to know what she'd said. She hadn't talked long. Just enough to beg us to give ourselves up to the authorities. We'd decided to take her advice: you can't spend a whole life running. On Sunday, the day the crowd surrounded us, Mariéla had chosen a new bike and paid for a complete tour of the square. Ordinarily, this would have meant riding the length of the square, heading off down the side of the Palais des Ministères, then turning left to pass in front of the social security office and the movie theater. Me, I just wanted to listen to the music. She had a right to her Sunday. If the crowd had waited, there wouldn't have been a scuffle. Of course they didn't forgive her for fighting all those people. Corazón talked to us all the time about how personal honor comes from inner strength. In his mouth, that was all lies, and women didn't count. To Mariéla, those words are true. Someone will have to think about warning all the poor beggars in the women's prison: Mariéla, she shows her claws if you don't leave her alone. She can be nice, though. The first day, a few minutes after that weird apathetic guy had left, Romulus spotted us on our bench. Filled with good intentions, without even suspecting what had happened (who would ever have imagined it?), he wanted to take us back home. He's only twenty-two and he's not physically strong. She could have stood up to him. Scratched him. Bitten him. Or challenged him with her fists. She didn't. Instead of attacking, she chose to kiss him. Although he's old enough to know about women, Romulus was completely staggered. And let us get away.

After the apathetic gentleman left, we were all alone, Mariéla and I. She asked me again if I was hungry, and I told her no. I was thinking that, on this evening at least, a curious public would once again have gathered in front of our house. Corazón's death was not a foreseeable misfortune. No one would ever have expected it. In the slum, however, there are certain voices that speak with authority and whose function is to predict catastrophe. Messengers of doom who sense the approach of floods and death. Not one had foretold the second death of Corazón. People would be annoyed at missing out on this unanticipated drama, at arriving after the removal of the body, too late to witness the tragedy, when there's nothing left to see or do except the poor consolation of gathering in groups to gossip late into the night. I personally would have liked to forget. Unfortunately, the event will mark a signal date in the history of the slum. More important than Christmas or our national commemoration day. Life, good or bad, doesn't interest people. It's death that makes a splash. Since we couldn't stay forever on that bench, Mariéla suggested that we continue on downtown. We prepared to leave. Suddenly, there was Romulus, Madame Jean-Baptiste's nephew, standing in front of us. A bit stiff and ill at ease in his usher's uniform. We'd hardly ever seen him in his working clothes, khaki gray with a black collar, and we hadn't recognized him among the throng of employees. He had found a job at the Ministry of the Interior and respected tradition: he no longer lived in the neighborhood. He shows up on Saturday afternoons, though, to play a few games of cards with his childhood friends. He's well liked, especially by older folks. The lucky ones, when they get the slightest promotion, they usually move far away and never come back. We meet them in the street and they don't recognize us. Romulus comes back to us every weekend, shaking hands with the oldsters to pay them his respects. And he smiles at everyone. Romulus has always been a serious boy. The more people said so, the more serious he was. He's the only youngster from the neighborhood who tried to live up to the idea we had of him. Romulus is the good example that no one else has followed. Even Joséphine, who hardly has enough energy to mind anyone else's business, used to repeat that to us all the time. Romulus is a good boy. Corazón didn't like her to say that. He took that praise for someone else as a personal insult. Everything Joséphine said, Corazón heard as a jibe or a complaint. Perhaps that's why she barely spoke at all, finally. That still hadn't satisfied Corazón. If she kept quiet, he heard even the silence, and found it full of reproach. Romulus is a good boy. Everyone agrees on that. It's true that he did everything for the best. He stayed in school until he got his certificate, and he doesn't run after girls. He even went and found himself a job, and without pulling any dubious strings to get it. His friends say he's girl-shy because he's turned tightfisted. I think they're jealous. It's not fun to look bad in comparison. On each visit, he doesn't shrink from lecturing them. "To get ahead in life, you have to manage carefully the little you've got." After he started working, he became a philosopher and now tacks "discipline and order" onto every sentence. At the ministry he took a thing called a training seminar, and now he constantly sounds as if he were reciting a lesson. But he has remained obliging and affectionate, always ready to help bring order to a situation. It was in the name of discipline that he stood there before us, with his questions. What are you doing here? Do your parents know where you are? And why are you carrying that bag? Plus a thousand and one questions that rained down on us. Questions without answers. We hadn't the heart to invent a reasonable explanation for him. Orderly people are quite tenacious, so tossing off a simple lie wouldn't have worked. We would have had to invent a detailed story on the spot, and it wouldn't have lasted more than an hour. That evening he would learn the truth and be annoyed at having been fooled by a couple of juvenile offenders. I began to babble. Mariéla stayed silent. Staring at him. Actually, I think it was the uniform she was looking at. He was staring at her, too. The questions were addressed to her. The principle of hierarchy—always that discipline and order—required that he speak to the older child. Then he noticed the bloodstains on the dress. I saw the fear in his eyes. His tone grew sterner, the interrogation more pointed. The bloodstains worried him. People remember blood only when someone, somewhere, has made the mistake of bleeding. People rarely think about the blood that can drain away on the inside. The blood that dries up beneath the skin. Mangy dogs wander through our neighborhood by the dozens at night. Now and then we find one just plain dead, with no clue as to what killed it. Except that it's bone-dry. You can poke thorns at the rigid hide all you want without raising a single drop of blood. A little like Joséphine. Before, when Corazón hit her, she bled from everywhere. From her pores, her nostrils. The lips, too, which took weeks to scar over. In the end, she didn't bleed at all. A bit of drool would dribble from her lips, that's all. People think it's a virtue to wince at seeing a single drop of blood. It isn't the wound that distresses them, it's the stain or the puddle soiling the decor, the floor, the clothing. Romulus is a man of order. He doesn't like excess. And blood on the dress of a sixteen-year-old girl sitting on a bench in the Champ-de-Mars with her little brother, at four in the afternoon, far from their native slum, that's something that's out of order. So he began to shout. You're bleeding? You were fighting? Whose blood is that on your dress? He looked at us as though we had murdered someone. Which was sort of true, after all: Mariéla had struck Corazón with the wrench, and I had held the giant's feet to make him tip over. But it was false, too. It wasn't anything we'd planned. The way we sometimes decided to play a trick on Fat Mayard or Stammering Jhonny. Or go steal fruit from some garden in the fancy neighborhoods. Or sneak into the Capitol movie theater to see a film for free. Romulus was convinced we'd done something terribly bad. Discipline and order required that he be a good citizen and inform our parents. Come, I'll take you home. He took my arm and began to push me gently along. Mariéla was dawdling behind us. From time to time he'd turn around to make sure she was still there. She pretended to be slowed down by the bag on her back. Me, I was launching futile kicks and coughing like an invalid. Passersby were stopping. Embarrassed by all the fuss, Romulus kept explaining. I work for the Ministry of the Interior. I have an ID card and a uniform. The crowd was on his side and ordered us to obey him. A man in a hurry yelled at him to haul off and spank us, pull us along by the hair, and well shit, just get it done. But Mariéla, although she's not tall, she already has her female figure, and other onlookers replied that she was too old to be spanked and that hitting, as everybody knows, is never good discipline. I got scared. Hitting, I'd had plenty of that. Between two swipes at Joséphine, I'd get one just in passing. Corazón had been so disappointed at having had a droopy, weakling son, dogged by malaria, instead of a robust athlete like himself. He'd never raised a hand to Mariéla. Luckily, Romulus applied discipline without preaching violence. He spoke like a teacher, calmly and firmly. Maybe they teach that technique in the training seminar. To chase away the beggars and job seekers blocking the entrance to the ministry. Go away. Don't stay there. Telephone to make an appointment. Come along. You must follow me. You have to understand that what I'm doing is for your own good. Joséphine worries about every little thing. Romulus kept dragging me along. Mariéla was following. She looked quite docile. I was still kicking out, however, and at last I got Romulus in the shin. Without really hurting him. But my recalcitrance had ticked him off. Goodbye, monsieur teacher! He was now a corporal, with a vocabulary limited to commands and dammit. Being a sentry and patrolling in khaki is enough to get you talking like an officer. Instead of hanging back, Mariéla was now almost running to catch up with us. When she got close to Romulus, she leaned close to his ear to tell him something confidential: The seams have come open in your uniform, there, take a look, under the arms. She said that without raising her voice. In a secretive tone, with the tenderness of an accomplice. But loud enough for passersby to hear. Romulus automatically lifted an arm to check. An orderly man does not wear a torn uniform. Seeing that the thread had indeed come undone in one armhole, he let go of my hand. He walked rigidly, keeping his arms close to his body. To remedy the flaw. And just like that, he could no longer find the words to give advice or issue commands. His arms still clamped to his sides, he spoke to us with his eyes. He'd been reduced to imploring us with his gaze. Help me do my duty. He seemed so unhappy that Mariéla did an amazing thing, to console him and effect our getaway. She took his hands, so very gently; he resisted, endeavoring to hide the torn garment. She forced him to lift his arms from his sides. She kissed him on the cheek and said, We can't go home. Not right away. Don't worry about your jacket, your aunt can sew it up for you. Then we took off, she and I, in the opposite direction. Toward the lower part of town. I turned around. Romulus's greatest virtue is his perseverance: he isn't the kind of man to abandon a chosen task for a trifle. But a kiss is not a trifle. He wasn't following us. Mariéla was smiling, radiantly. He was still rooted in the same spot, looking dazed, caressing the sweet memory of lips brushing his cheek. He saw me watching him and recovered his personality. He about-faced like a military recruit on parade. Then he vanished into the crowd, walking stiffly, looking straight ahead, arms glued to his sides.

We walked toward the lower part of town. Toward the sea. Leaving the big administrative buildings behind. We passed neighborhoods we hardly knew at all, except for Bas Peu de Chose, where Corazón was born.[4] Before she left, Mam Yvonne used to visit us when she felt like it. She'd walk in whenever she pleased, arriving at times when no one expected her. Crossing the alleyways, taking care to pick her way through the trash scattered almost everywhere. In the house, she took off her walking shoes and put on another pair she always carried in her purse. When it was time to go, she'd switch back to her going-visiting shoes. When she went by, women gave her dirty looks and hoodlums whistled at her. No one dared push the mockery any further. Mam Yvonne thought that she intimidated them. She had no idea that if she hadn't been Corazón's mother, people would have set traps for her, strewn her path with fruit pits and banana peels. In the slum, no one trusts visitors. People might have doused her pretty dress with basins of our running water, the black water of our thousand needs: laundry, food, washing out wounds. Mam Yvonne did not belong in the shantytown alleys. Either in the alleys or in our house. She stuck out. Even more than Filsien, Marcel's half brother, who'd turned twenty while still in primary school. Every year he failed the exams for the certificate. He could have kept going for a long time, despite the laughter and his beard. One day he saw his face in a class photo. The picture showed him that his place was not among this tribe of kiddies who giggled behind his back and called him Papa. Filsien had taken some time to figure things out. Mam Yvonne still hadn't. Too busy looking at us and feeling sorry for us, too busy trying to get Corazón to see reason the way she saw it in Bas Peu de Chose. But she never saw how we saw her. To our neighbors, she was more than an oddity—she was a living insult. Everyone shunned us. While she was visiting us, no neighbor lady would come borrow soap or the frying pan. The lottery players avoided dropping in to discuss the previous day's results with Corazón. The other poor people left us alone with the stranger. Joséphine tied herself in knots to be nice to her, behaving as though we lived in a real house, as though we had the means to entertain guests. In the presence of Mam Yvonne, Joséphine tried to act rich. To please Corazón, who insisted that we had everything we needed: Things are going fine at the garage, I'm well paid, and the children are doing well. Joséphine and I were forced to say the same thing. Only Mariéla said nothing. No word was worth it. They were just phrases with no future. A lot of useless lies. In moments of crisis, when things got really tough, Mariéla and I would go see Mam Yvonne. Our faces, our shoes, our beggar-child embarrassment told her all about our real life, erasing every lie trotted out the day before. On our way there, Mariéla would advise me not to answer any questions. The right answers, however, earned candies. The worse things were, the more candies we got. We were still fairly young. Today Mariéla turns men's heads. Back when we were visiting Mam Yvonne, no one paid us any attention. Except when I coughed. Sometimes I did it on purpose to terrorize the passersby. The first time we went, Joséphine showed us the way. She'd waited for us, out in the street, hidden behind a tree. Corazón had forbidden any member of his family to set foot in Mam Yvonne's house. Following Joséphine's logic, children could disobey their father, but the wife had to obey her husband. Joséphine has always been a most dutiful wife. Sometimes things went just great. For a few hours. A few days, maximum. If he'd won at the lottery. Corazón taught us boxing and would take Mariéla in his arms to whirl her around like a top. Then something would happen to aggravate him. Either my clumsiness, or Joséphine's tears. I have to say, Joséphine cried all year round. We didn't have enough money, and she had debts to pay off. But none of the families in the neighborhood have ever had enough money. And all poor people, luckily, do not fight among themselves. In our house, the punches, the screaming, the quarrels and prayers were the finishing touch to our poverty. Corazón would go into a rage for some reason and stay there for weeks. At the worst moments, Joséphine looked older than Mam Yvonne, and sadder. Mam Yvonne wasn't sad, just running out of patience. One day she came to propose that we follow her to the United States. Corazón replied that he didn't need anyone's help to take care of his family. That day she yelled at him that he was a brute, a fool, and a forty-year-old failure who didn't even have a decent job or home. Thank God your father isn't here anymore to see this. Mam Yvonne seemed possessed of unshakable strength. And big, too. Almost as big as her giant of a son. When we went to her house, she would welcome us on the threshold, drawing us gently inside her home. After she'd closed the door behind us, I felt a great comfort, mixed with uneasiness. The comfort of finding myself in a house with real rooms, a toilet, and a chandelier. Uneasiness at seeing pity in her eyes. You'd have thought she saw the very color of misfortune in Mariéla's messy hair and my pimply skin. I appreciated being spoiled, but the despair in her eyes upset me. Mariéla often threw the gifts our poverty had inspired into the sewer drains. The problem with going to rich people's homes is that they know as well as you do that it's want that brings you there. Never fear, I'll leave you everything. If only Colin would agree . . . One day she'd had enough. She left to live with our great-aunt, saying that the country had changed so much she no longer recognized it and that the entire family would do better to follow her. Corazón didn't want to. She also said she'd keep helping us from over there, while she waited for us to be able to decide for ourselves. And Corazón shouted that he hoped to live a long time, and as long as I live

I'll be the head of this family! On that day Mam Yvonne grew suddenly old. The words flying by dropped years on her, and at the end of the conversation, despite her clean shoes and her complete sentences, she looked like the moribund grandmothers withering away in the shantytown. A grandmother, in our neighborhood, that's an old lady with rotten teeth or none at all who waits for someone to get around to feeding her, parking her in the warming sun like a rancid rag, washing her in public to the amusement of onlookers. Our slum's a place without grandparents. Unless you count a few corpses forgotten by the passage of time. Ancient mummies reduced by poverty and brain collapse to the state of infants. I remember Sor Lucienne, Fat Mayard's great-aunt. She'd open her mouth, you'd see a big black hole, but no trace of a tooth. Everybody avoided her. Including her great-nephews. She didn't do a thing for herself. You had to hold her spoon, and force her to bathe. As soon as she saw the bucket, the old woman started shrieking and would crawl naked as an earthworm all the way to the shortcut leading to the furniture factory. You had to run after her, wrestle her back, and wash her down long-distance by emptying the bucket at her. The old lady hated water and struggled so much she sometimes had to be tied up. One day, she died. Her family, as was customary, observed the usual mourning. But basically, everyone was happy. Having her on their hands, complaining constantly, that wasn't a life, either for her or for them. A grandmother, she's a burden, a trial, a wreck. Mam Yvonne was the exception. On the day of her last visit, Corazón said, My children aren't going anywhere. I'm their father, and I'm the one who decides. Since then Mam Yvonne has been an orphaned grandmother. I felt sad for her. I mean, it was nice of her to offer us everything she has. She was a little pitiful. But not as much as Joséphine. That one was pitiful every day of the year. Off in her house in Bas Peu de Chose, without being one hundred percent jolly, Mam Yvonne didn't seem unhappy to us. She'd fix us doughnuts, and fritters called *accras* made from grated malanga root, hot peppers, and black-eyed peas. She tried to teach me to talk without swearing, and when I said silly things, it made her laugh. She also showed us photos of Corazón. In lots of them he's only a baby, without any real features or personality. In others, he's wearing a bad-boy look. Sometimes his eyes are closed. My favorite is his cowboy photo, with a hat and a pair of pistols. He doesn't really look mean on the wooden horse. He's sulking. Mam Yvonne told us how she loved to sing him a song about a snail. Maybe when he grew up he stayed a child, an old baby snail with fists as big as his head. Mam Yvonne also said that he'd cried for weeks, wanting his father to find him a wooden horse like the one in the photo. Unfortunately, there was only one wooden horse in the whole country, so Mam Yvonne and her husband had offered to buy the photographer's unique model, he had only to name the price. The photographer had turned them down, on behalf of the other little children who also longed to sit astride the horse. It's in that photo that I love Corazón the best. He looks like Mariéla. Going through the pictures in order, you can watch him grow up. Beneath the last photo in the album, Mam Yvonne wrote in a careful hand, "Fifteen years old." "That's how old he was when he left to try his luck in the Dominican Republic," she said. "When he took that idiotic nickname of Corazón. Fifteen—that's the age of foolishness. His real name is Colin. Colin Pamphile, like you." She would hand us an envelope for Joséphine and shoo us out before evening came. Mam Yvonne was not afraid of anything, except the twilight. We'd hear her bolt the door behind us. If Corazón hadn't been so stubborn, the house would have come to him. He didn't want it. When Joséphine mentioned the word "inheritance" and talked about our rights, he started pounding. Back then I thought "inheritance" was a serious insult. Mariéla explained to me what the word meant. I didn't understand why Corazón objected to the idea of living in Mam Yvonne's house. Who can love poverty? It's a real house. A little run-down, of course, like everything that lives in the neighborhood of Bas Peu de Chose. The studio where Corazón had his beautiful cowboy photo taken still exists, with the same blue backdrop, the same owner. I went inside once. I left without having a picture taken—the lovely wooden horse is gone. Everything's old in Bas Peu de Chose. And a lot quieter than our neighborhood. Coming back from Mam Yvonne's, until we left Bas Peu de Chose and came out on the Place des Héros, we'd hardly see any young people in the streets. Just old folks. You'd have thought it was a rendezvous for retirees. Whereas out by us there are so many undertwenties that for our holiday championships, we've got almost as many teams as the national league. On the evening of Corazón's death, Bas Peu de Chose seemed the same as always. I felt comforted by the familiar surroundings. In my first statement, I described our itinerary. The officers had asked for that. A detective concluded that Mam Yvonne's house was the coveted object that had driven us to commit the crime. Mam Yvonne's house? We walked past without looking at it. Without thinking about it. It's not correct to say that we succumbed to temptation. Mariéla and I have always had dreams. But very few plans. When we were little, the only thing we really cared about was to go to the amusement park with lots of tokens. And to have enough pocket money for a Sunday on the square. Where they have ice cream, and bike rides. Later, Mariéla changed dreams. She wanted to go to the ends of the earth, live a real life. Relying on her own strength. We never talked about the house. The evening Corazón died, we didn't have enough stamina to have any ideas. To think about the future. And Mariéla, I can say this, has never relied on others. She wouldn't ever lay one finger on anything belonging to someone else. She's proud, like Corazón, but he said all those fine things without putting them into practice. He wound up begging, imploring, borrowing without repaying, intercepting mail that wasn't addressed to him. As I told the police, me, the only thing I dreamed of that evening as we walked through Bas Peu de Chose—it wasn't very smart, but it wasn't a crime, either—was that old wooden horse Corazón rode on for his cowboy photo.

W e walked down to the lower part of the city. To the train tracks. Mam Yvonne had often spoken to us of the railroad that once linked cities together. Of the Parisiana Theater, where great actors and actresses had appeared. Of the sea that was driven out when the state-owned stores were built. Of the palm trees. And the tracks. Most of what Mam Yvonne talked about seemed known only to her, so that I wondered if she might be inventing a past custom-made to make the present look bad. A past with trains, circuses, flower shows, and other unbelievable things that didn't go with the dusty landscape in which we'd grown up. If Mam Yvonne were to be trusted, it was as if there were two cities in a single one. Two dead cities, back to back. Ours is a city with its feet in the dirt, a black city without head or tail. Mam Yvonne's city lives, invisibly, on the bright side of memory. It left its train tracks behind, along with the bougainvillea. We couldn't tell whether the ancient automobiles lined up all along the track bed had been parked there or simply abandoned. You'd have thought it was a cemetery where scrap iron came to die. There were only very old models with faded paintwork. Cars that were dead, or in a bad way. I know a little something about cars. Marcel and Stammering Jhonny and I, we used to play at identifying cars from their sound. Each engine has its own way of expressing itself, its own voice, its breath. Marcel would climb onto the roof of the furniture factory, at the entrance to the shantytown. The furniture factory is our only open door onto the city outside. The only neighborhood building over-looking a real street. From its roof, Marcel could see cars going by. A harmless challenge, just a game, a pastime—we didn't have any money to really bet with. Jhonny and I had to tell which cars were passing from the noise they made. We never won. Marcel had invented the game and always claimed the privilege of being the one to climb up to the roof. Every time we thought we'd got it, he'd yell down from his perch that we were wrong again. We were sure he was cheating. One day we decided to catch him in the act. We fol-lowed him onto the roof. It was the first time I'd ever climbed that high. Things don't look the same from the earth and the sky. From the front, the cars looked smaller. In the rear view, the gray roofs of the neigh-borhood shacks were all lined up like peanut shells. Hearing us come up behind him, Marcel turned around and gave us a goofy smile. To apologize. He smiled and did a crazy thing. Took a big step into the void as though he were going to fly. And then he fell. Still looking at us. It didn't kill him. He came out of it with a broken arm, but we never played that game again. In the middle of a soccer match or while he's standing there, in living color in front of me, laughing or telling some story, I see it again, him falling from the furniture factory roof. The same thing happens to Jhonny, despite what his mother tells us. She keeps trying to convince us that Marcel fell because he was pushed by his guilty conscience. "Nothing happens without a reason—the proverbs tell us so: the wicked man always trips over his evil deeds." We felt a bit responsible for Marcel's fall. Ever since, we've let him cheat as he pleases. At any game at all, even the most harmless ones. The furniture factory is very big. We're all proud of it. It's our only building worthy of the other neighborhoods, with its double door, the workshop at street level, and the office on the first floor. Marcel, he fell from high up, and by all rights he should have broken his neck. Since his fall everyone calls him "the Bird" or "Miracle Boy," and no one wants to annoy or upset him so as not to overstrain his luck. The evening of Corazón's death, while we were walking by the tracks, I wasn't thinking about my friends. I was really too tired to think at all, and only began obsessing about them the following day. Mariéla picked a car at random and we collapsed onto the back seat, which was off its supports and creaked like a box mattress. Both of us were tired. Mariéla refused that defeat and strove to keep her eyes wide open so that nothing and no one would take us by surprise. I tried to imitate her. She took off her sandals and dug her nails into the canvas of the bag. To get rid of the tension. We stayed there awhile without talking, looking around on all sides. Without seeing anything besides the night. A few stars. Some stray dogs. And the dark shapes of cars. Then I suggested the question game. Mariéla invented it to help me go over my schoolwork for exams. I would ask her the question, she would read me the correct answer and toss the question back at me. All I had to do was repeat what she'd said. Three times, ten times. That's how I was able to memorize the names of a few inventors and some rules about numbers. And reel off some big wars with grand battles you have to know by heart, and some really small ones with less studied deaths that get only a paragraph at the end of a chapter. And some harder lessons. About plants and snakes. It made Joséphine happy to know that I'd been promoted to the next grade. Mariéla and I hadn't played that game since I'd stopped going to school. That evening, it was for real. The answers weren't written in books. To find meaning in life, or death, we couldn't just settle for ready-made truths from schoolbooks. There wasn't any reward. No good points, no promotions. No proud smile on Joséphine's face, no prayers of thanksgiving, because you owe everything to God, including your health and intelligence. That evening, we had to invent. Find out who we were. Overcome Corazón's death. Escape or accept it. Break the thread. Or mend it. Come up with a language that could say everything. That would hold the past, the present, and the future together. We had to be the same as we'd been the day before. Or learn that we had changed, that from then on we would speak only words without a unifying thread, only free-floating sentences, just good for killing time. We had a bit of money and some useless things. A few stars in the sky and some drifting words that could no longer help us. Or Mam Yvonne, fresh out of heirs. Or Joséphine, who hadn't learned to live without the thought of a man in her bed. Or Corazón, whom we'd killed, sort of by accident, sort of on purpose. Words that weren't true, or false. Were we right to do what we did? I don't know. What do you think? I don't know either. I mean about running away? I don't know. Won't they believe that it was something we wanted to do for a long time, that we prepared for like an exam or a party? I don't know. Anyway, we can't change what people think. People think without knowing. You remember when Filidor was accused of cutting the power lines to sell them at the flea market, and everyone agreed it was him? Yes, I remember. Squads armed with clubs and carrying torches caught the real thieves. But people had already chosen Filidor to play the role of thief, and they didn't want to change their minds. So he went off someplace where people wouldn't think badly of him. Does everyone have to think the same thing? I don't think so. Everybody's free to choose. Sometimes everyone agrees on the same thing, to avoid arguments. It must make them feel more comfortable to all have the same opinion. It's true you don't get yourself into shit when you repeat what everyone else says. Are they going to lock us up? I mean in a prison or a reformatory? I don't know. Yes, probably. And will we be locked up together? I don't know. But we'll always be together. And Joséphine, what will she think? Maybe she won't see things the way the others will, since she's all alone now? Joséphine, she won't think anything, she'll just stick with suffering and let God think for her. Sometimes I wonder if she isn't happy suffering all the time. Joséphine . . . Why are you angry at her? I don't know. Maybe because she doesn't exist . . . If they lock us up, do you think she'll forget us and go find someone who'll beat her like Corazón? I don't think so. Corazón, she really loved him. Like people worship the cross or have themselves whipped to imitate Christ. Joséphine, she's doomed to spend her life dying. And Corazón, do you think he forgives us? Corazón's dead. Not just inside his head, like zombies and Joséphine. Dead, for real. And the dead don't have the power anymore to forgive or to beg forgiveness. Do you think he loved us? I don't know. Yes, I think he did love us. You. Because you're a strong girl. Do you think he loved me, though? I don't know. I think so, even if he didn't know it himself. How can you know when you love someone? You feel it. I miss him, here. I miss them both. If we could erase everything . . . You can't erase everything. Why did he beat her? I don't know. He only talked about it when he was drunk . . . "It isn't me, it's my hands . . ." A kind of rage that takes over the head and comes out through the fists. Now that he's dead, we have to tell ourselves that it wasn't him, but a strength or a weakness that can't listen to reason. And us, do you think we've got that rage in our hands? I don't know. You, no. I mean, a kind of force that pushes us, that's too strong for us? I don't know. But if it isn't something that just happened on its own, if we wanted his death, are we maybe murderers? We're all so barely alive, I mean the people in the neighborhood. Maybe we should all die and let the cacti take over. Are we murderers? I don't know what we are. Are we murderers? I don't know what we are. Are we murderers? I don't know what . . .

In those days, Jesus was already famous, and everyone awaited his arrival in Cana. The next day, it was the preacher's voice that woke us. The voice filled the street, rousing the fear that slept in us. *Jesus was already famous, and everyone awaited his arrival in Cana.* There was only the man with his parables. Bible, detachable collar, and megaphone. Not even the sun. Just the coolness of early morning, and the sky now empty of stars. Day had not yet broken, with its heat and filth. Yet the man of God was perspiring. Big drops ran down his face. All preachers perspire, whatever the season. When there's a good crowd in attendance, the minister of the Baptist church has a disciple who follows him with a handkerchief to pat his brow during the pause after each Amen. The preacher of the railroad tracks was revved up on his own, like a machine running on empty, without a hankie or a congregation. He tapped his foot at every phrase, keeping time. The God who shouts in the street in poor people's neighborhoods doesn't follow the slow rhythm of the

Lord of churches. The preacher was hopping around. They say that's a technique that lets you crush evil underfoot. *The righteous awaited the master to venerate and obey him. But there was also the host of unbelievers, come to provoke him.* In our neighborhood, we too have preachers launched into the early morning to bear witness to their faith. Ours are sure of finding an audience. Where we live, no matter what time it is, we never run out of people. The slightest noise gets them up and outside, like an army. The railroad preacher was laboring in a void, his eye on all four horizons, waiting for a passerby to save his sermon. *The crowd had learned that the master was coming to the wedding. The betrothed were among his friends, and he had promised to come to Cana to serve as their witness. Knowing that the Lord always keeps his promises, curious onlookers had gathered before the entrance to the house where the reception was being held.* His wedding wasn't like Joséphine's. But I suppose God has a word for each of us. And what does it matter, anyway? I thought of Corazón's death. God couldn't be on our side. By moving discreetly to avoid drawing the preacher's attention, we changed into clean clothes. Mariéla drew the bloodstained dress off over her head. She wasn't wearing a bra, she never does. And I was able to see how much her body had changed since our childhood. Even since that night we'd danced close together. Her body was more of a body. Her breasts had grown. Her young woman's breasts, as Joséphine said in her martyr's voice, to show her disapproval. Joséphine had taken this bra business so seriously that she'd talked to Corazón about it. That was a kind of betrayal. In general, instinctively, we all three protected ourselves by not telling him anything about the thoughts or actions of the other two. Joséphine, too weak, often violated our pact. She'd talked to him about the bra problem because, She's a woman now, with males prowling around her breasts. But Corazón never paid attention to such details. All he asked of us was not to get in his way. And he had a soft spot for Mariéla. He admired her strength and her independence. She was his son. Me, he'd put me in the same class as Joséphine, with the weaklings ripe for massacre. He was furious with me when the doctor announced that I had malaria and was too sickly to take up boxing. *The crowd had entered the house of the betrothed couple. Informed of the presence of Jesus, strangers who were not on the guest list had entered the house to join the celebration. The godly among the throng had followed our Lord to touch him and to gaze upon him. For to see Jesus in the living flesh is the purest of graces. But the mass of unbelievers had come to defy him. There were several false prophets who set a bad example and taunted him. When will you finally prove that you are the son of God? If what you claim is true, work a miracle for us here and now! They had agreed among themselves to humiliate our Lord. They laid a snare for him. They decided to waste the wine, to dry up the casks.* I had stupidly thrown my pants from yesterday into the bag without remembering to remove our money from my pocket. The pants had slipped to the bottom of the bag, so the easiest way to get them was to empty the bag. I pulled the clothing out. A blouse, a shirt from when Mam Yvonne was still here . . . But I couldn't lay hands on the money. Suddenly, way at the bottom, I touched something silky. Something as soft as sin. I jerked back, and the movement caught the attention of the preacher. He finally spotted us and smiled in satisfaction. Happy to have an audience, he followed the tracks to our car. Laying his voice upon us. Using his megaphone to its maximum effect. *So then the unbelievers and wicked men began to waste the wine. The women and children who did not usually drink any followed the men's example by pouring the wine into their cups and tossing it out the window. The men drank of it greedily. They bribed the servants, who tipped over full pitchers with hypocritical smiles. And when the wine was all gone . . .* We got out of the door that opened onto the sidewalk, and he stopped right by the left-hand door, out in the street. We stood there on either side of the car. He shouted through his megaphone about all the misdeeds of the unbelievers who had broached the casks of wine to humiliate Jesus. Mariéla told him to bugger off and leave us alone, to go take his sermon to a busier street. The preacher heard only the voice of God, however, and soon added us to his list of unbelievers. Fortunately, other people were showing up with the sunrise. A group of men appeared at the other end of the street. Four of them. One was in blue overalls like Corazón's, but dirtier; the other three were in T-shirts and grease-stained trousers wearing out at the knees. They were mechanics. Real ones. Not copies like Corazón. That was when we realized our mistake: the street along the railroad tracks was not a used-car cemetery at all, but a garage along its whole length. An open-air garage for cars so old that probably no one would want them anymore, except their owners. The vehicle we had spent the night in had not been abandoned, and if the mechanics found our bag on the seat, they might think we were thieves. *And when the wine was all gone, the crowd of unbelievers went straight up to Jesus and said to him with one voice, "You who claim to work miracles, will you let your friends end their wedding without anything to drink, either for themselves or for the assembled company? And what is a wedding where only bread and water are served to the guests? Is this how the god you claim to be comes to the aid of his friends? Make wine for us, if you are God. Their voices dripped with sarcasm. And Jesus, seeing through the trick, would not have replied to their provocations except for the urging of his disciples and dozens of the admirers who had come to see him. So, pointing to the casks that the unbelievers had drained to the last drop, he said, "Look ye not there, for whosoever thinks he knows the intentions of the true God will always be surprised by his omnipotence . . ."* The grease monkeys did not make a good audience: they set to work without paying any attention to the preacher, inspecting the cars one after the other, opening the doors, taking spare parts and tools out from under the seats—jacks, and wrenches even bigger than the one that . . . The man in overalls came over to our car and saw the bag in the back seat. I hadn't managed to get the pants out, and they still contained all our money. The rest wasn't important: a bloodstained dress, some poorly made clothing that we'd been wearing forever—nothing worth clinging to, no great loss. Except that item so soft to the touch that had lighted a sweet fire in my hand. The man opened the bag to check its contents, throwing our clothes into the street as they came to hand. He didn't throw away the panties. How can such a small thing have such a big effect? The man touched them as though they were a promise, and I felt what he was feeling. Pretty. A delicate green. Mariéla's favorite color. Not at all like the big cotton underpants the neighborhood ladies wear. A real pair of pretty girl's panties, as dainty as a secret. There are some like it in the R-rated movies we sometimes watch when there aren't any action films. The man turned toward us and stared right at Mariéla. With a look that didn't hide a thing. That went straight to the point. A rutting animal, undressing Mariéla, putting on her little panties, and taking them off. The man called to his friends, who answered him vaguely while they continued working. Captivated by the charming panties, the preacher was taking a short break. Then, *Jesus addressed the crowd and said, pointing to the casks of water, "See, there is where you will find the wine." The Lord spoke to them without having to raise his voice. And everyone heard him: "In the house of my friends and the servants of my father, there is always enough to quench the thirst of men of good will. Serve yourselves, the casks are full." Everyone thronged into the banquet hall. The unbelievers as well as the faithful crowded around the casks and found them full of the most delicious wine. The best from the vine, for God offers us only things of quality.* The mechanics asked the preacher to shut up because they had work to do. The one in the overalls, however, had eyes only for Mariéla. Mariéla in her panties. Mariéla naked. Mariéla like in the movies. And I saw what he was seeing. If you want them, girlie, you have to earn them. One cuddle, and I'll give them back to you. Annoyed by the whole business, the other mechanics tried to calm him down: They're only kids, just let them go. But he kept at it, trying to speak louder than the preacher, who was still ranting. *The Lord offers us only quality products. Seduced by the taste of the wine and the miracle of abundance, the unbelievers, admitting defeat* . . . If you want them, girlie, you have to earn them: just one cuddle and I'll give you back your panties, and your bag . . . *joined their voices to the concert of praise. And Jesus calmed the crowd and sent the people home, because our Lord is not a star who hungers for applause, and the newlyweds needed to be alone* . . . One kiss and I'll give them back. I'm sure you're a little slut. Mariéla was shaking with fury. I was looking for stones. Nothing, no weapon. Nothing but the useless lines of the tracks and the asphalt. And the man was brandishing the panties, waving them around in the morning breeze. And the preacher was running with sweat, intoxicated by his wine, his wedding, and the unquenchable verve of his performance. So since the preacher, drunk on the Lord's wine, was looking at us without seeing us, I clambered over the car, grabbed his megaphone, and threw it at the mechanic's head. I missed. My aim is never very good, and when we played with slingshots I never hit the targets. Not even the biggest ones, like buzzards and screech owls. The outraged mechanic came after me. The preacher saved Mariéla and me by trying to get his megaphone back. The two of them rushed forward without seeing one another and there was a glorious collision, the preacher toppling the mechanic, both of them falling as one, rolling across the tracks, legs all tied up in their joint tussle, scissoring open and shut in the dust of the tracks, finally untangling, each man standing up apart from the other, whom he accused of knocking him down, the preacher clasping his megaphone to his breast like a mother cradling her child, the mechanic wild with anger, the panties no longer a trophy in his hands, just something to help dust himself off. There was no way to get them back. During the mix-up, I'd had time only to recover the money, and now, to start off our second day, we ran as fast as we had the day before. Without any destination, plan, or objective. Leaving behind Corazón's body, Joséphine's lamentations, the memory of Mam Yvonne, and our outgrown clothes. And Mariéla's panties, her present to herself, perhaps the only thing that was worth carrying away with us. Behind us we could hear the voices of the now quarreling men, the preacher affirming that *The Lord sends us trials equal to our faith*, the mechanic vowing to bring the man of God back to earth by making him swallow his damned megaphone, and the other mechanics laughing at their antics as they scolded their colleague: But we told you to leave those kids alone! Young ones like that, they bring bad luck, especially the girls, and we truly told you so! Such girls are magnets for trouble . . .

Our fortune amounted to about sixty gourdes. Three bills and some coins. Sums like that did not hang around the house for long. Corazón usually helped himself freely to the week's reserves. Without any real fear of being caught, he would wait until Joséphine's back was turned, then stretch a long arm over the radio to open the jar. He would get up in the middle of the night, dress quietly, empty the jar, and leave without closing the door behind him. Actually, the place is so small that no one can do a thing without the others knowing. You hear everything. Corazón would open the curtain, step quickly into our half of the room, and look for the chest of drawers. Joséphine always left the jar in the same place. To make it easier for him. We would clearly hear him turning the jar lid with a practiced hand. He worked quickly; there were no bars in the shantytown, and he didn't like to drink standing in front of the stalls selling the harsh white rum called *clairin*, so he had to go elsewhere. And there was the lottery. The need to try his luck.

Sometimes he was in such a rush that coins would fall and roll across the floor—a racket to raise the dead. Joséphine would wake up with a start, and seeing Corazón hunched over, feeling around in the dark for the missing money, she would immediately close her eyes again to pretend she hadn't noticed anything. The next day, deathly sad and seeking the thief where she could never find him, she would look questioningly at the jar, then at me, then at Mariéla, but not at Corazón. Looking from the smallest to the biggest. Without getting to Corazón. Who would act as though he hadn't the foggiest idea what was going on. Dignified and indifferent, like an honest citizen refusing to become involved in a scandal or a crime. Right, I'm going out. Joséphine would simply say a prayer, and that was our food for the day. Or else she'd dip into our real reserves, beneath her mattress. If there was nothing there, then there was nothing in the house, and we were seriously poor. Corazón didn't know about this secret stash, but the jar—you'd have thought Joséphine kept it in plain sight on the chest just so's he could help himself. The two of them used to play competitive games like this, to see which of them was the best at his or her role. They had, so to speak, their areas of agreement. On the day he died—I know I ought to say, on the day we killed him—Corazón had not been into the jar. Anticipating the arrival of the mailman, he had set out the glasses for a discussion of Joe Louis. Joe: the best, Joe who never let down his guard, Joe who didn't dance around, didn't slink away. Joe, bravest of the brave. The hero of the ring. Who dished it out. Took it. Took it. Dished it out. Joe, about whom no one could say a bad word. One day, feeling his alcohol, the mailman opened a more personal vein of conversation. Speaking familiarly, as if they'd been old friends since forever, he told Corazón, That champion of yours goes back to the days of black and white and you've got no TV, so you don't know today's fighters. Your Joe wouldn't last long against the lousiest of these hefty boxers stuffed with vitamins and electronically trained. Corazón, he raised his massive fist and slammed it down on the table. The mailman swallowed his spit; the glass fell from his hand. To hide his fear he stayed a few minutes more, talking about anything at all except boxing and Joe Louis. Then he tried to leave. Corazón insisted that he stay. The man left anyway, saying that he had mail to deliver. He was walking fast, backwards. But Corazón summoned him again, loudly, and the mailman didn't dare disobey. Corazón gave him a whopping thump on the back to show him that nothing had changed but, Trust me, Joe Louis was the best, a real man, that guy. Corazón was always making grand gestures. Even his smiles were huge. Corazón did everything in a big way. His only weakness was hitting Joséphine, but you could see that simply as an overflow of strength. That's why for us, he died not in the house, murdered by his children, but shortly before, at the garage, when he became so small, without strength or dignity, without saying one word to defend himself when the boss—a half-decrepit shrimp not even a baby would see as a big man—was calling him all sorts of names. And the whole while Corazón just shook his head stupidly, humble as a beggar, even meeker than Joséphine. He wasn't Joe, or Corazón. Just a bunch of flabby muscles deflating under a heap of insults. Joe the wheelbarrow, Joe the car jack, only good for lifting heavy auto parts, Do what you're told seeing as that's all you can handle, and watch out if you try playing street magician one more time with an engine or a transmission. Corazón, heavy lifter, but mechanic? No way. And all those wrenches in his tool box, his blue overalls, those workdays he'd tell us about, his pride at being the only one to have understood why a transmission had seized up, why the rear wheels of a brand-new 4x4, fresh from the dealer's, had frozen solid. And the compliments from the clients, the other employees' jealousy, and the fact that he didn't have a fixed salary but received a percentage of every repair job—We didn't get much work this week, it's the slow season—and the tips those satisfied clients slipped into his pocket. It was easy to figure out how that money coincided with the remittances sent by Mam Yvonne: the clients at the garage were very generous after a visit from the mailman. So, like the boss was yelling, maybe there had never been any fight in the Dominican Republic, or even an El Negro to KO him in the ring. Nothing but a cane cutter or a provincial pimp, a complete fake. A vulgar small-time operator without the heart to tell the truth and who had people call him Corazón, "Heart," when his real name was Colin Pamphile, unmasked as Shame-on-You-Colin, Colin of the most pathetic pages in the sad book of proverbs, Colin the Has-been, Colin the Loser. The biggest lies come from furthest away.

The first day, I'd promised myself to live with the hunger. To wait for Mariéla. Time had put paid to my resolution. That's one thing I share with Corazón: our good intentions can't last long. On the morning of the second day, my hunger was bigger than my sense of honor. I had promised to wait for Mariéla, but what's a promise without witnesses? I was ready to give in, to yell at her to stop some place, and that it was all her fault, anyway. On the morning of the second day I was ready to talk from my stomach. Luckily, Mariéla didn't ask my opinion, she just decided that we needed to find something to eat. The hunger problem was going to be solved. I was furious, however, at always being one step behind her. We'd wandered around a long time after our run-in with the mechanic and the preacher. The morning was drawing to a close. To eat, all we had to do was head toward the industrial zone, where women sold hot meals to the factory workers. We had quite a selection, and out of respect for Mam Yvonne, we picked the vendor whose business looked the cleanest. The food on the fire was protected by a big strip of plastic that covered all the cooking pots, and the stall was at some distance from the street, in a kind of shed, away from the dust and dirty water thrown up by the passage of enormous trucks used for public transportation. The other vendors had set up their businesses right on the sidewalk. Mam Yvonne would not have considered these few steps from the street a sufficient guarantee of cleanliness. Mam Yvonne washed her hands before every meal. She said that back in her day, at least there was a Minister of Health worthy of the title. And now the street has turned into a kitchen. If only Colin . . . She still called him Colin, but we knew only Corazón. Maybe Colin existed in another era, with a mother who worked in the public sector, with education and good manners. A father who tried to get him the toys he asked for. As for Corazón, he ate that street food with the other garage employees while he told them about Joe Louis. Mam Yvonne advised us not to imitate him. Don't ever buy anything in the street. Mam Yvonne, she was talking to the wrong children in the wrong language, the one she'd used with Corazón when he was our age. Corazón, he had a choice, he could have eaten at home, with a table and cutlery, and parents to spoil him, but for us, things in the street—they're not a rebellion or a personal decision, they simply cost a lot less. Mariéla calculated that we could each buy a meal without spending all our resources. On the menu were white rice, boiled vegetables, chopped meat, and a chunk of sweet potato. Most of the workers ate standing up. And quickly. A few had set up some bricks and small planks taken from the debris of a house that was being torn down, and they ate more slowly, trying to balance on their improvised benches. Before serving us, the lady wanted to make sure that we could pay for our food: Some kids have already pulled that one on me. Standing with her face to the breeze, she busily doled out the portions. One ladleful of sauce, two serving spoons of white rice, another ladle for the vegetables and meat. After each serving, she briskly covered up her wares again to keep the dust from settling in her pots. When his meal was finished, each worker left his bowl and spoon on a small bench. A little girl would rinse the utensils in a basin and hand them to the vendor, who wiped them on her apron and served her next customer. The girl tended the fire and chased away the dogs eyeing the stewpan of meat. You kids, you'll have to wait. These gentlemen are in a hurry, and they're my best customers. I like clients who come regularly. The workers reacted to her courtesies with grunts and snubs. Don't bother pretending you like us—every month you raise your prices and reduce your portions. One day I'll win the lottery and treat myself to a real restaurant. No, don't say that, say instead that when you get to be boss, one evening you'll invite us with our wives and children to a blowout dinner at Le Tiffany, to make us forget all those extra hours of work. Speaking of women and children, seems there was a tragedy over by Fort National. Two kids killed their father. It was on the radio. I was looking for the sports news. More proof, just like I was telling you: got to watch out for children. You raise them the right way, but you can't control how they feel . . . We ate our money's worth and didn't let ourselves be bothered by the conversation. I tossed the bone to the dogs. I've always liked dogs. But it wasn't a good idea: there was a fight, and the strongest dog beat out the others, who were left looking at me in reproach for having created an illusion that turned into defeat. The workers drove them off. They hadn't paid good money to have stray dogs disrupting their meal. After checking that we were solvent, the vendor offered us some juice, but we preferred a can of Coca-Cola. The food, fine: like lemon, fire is a disinfectant. In our neighborhood, that's what housewives use to treat wounds. Juice, though . . . Without being as strict as Mam Yvonne about hygiene, Mariéla decided against it. The vendor was right: you give birth to children, but not to their feelings. If Mariéla hadn't been there I would have drunk the juice in a second, even knowing that the water probably came from a nearby ditch or from a bucket with a thousand other uses. I'm fairly easygoing. Someone tells me to leave, I leave. Someone tells me, eat, I eat. Without bothering to think about it. In any case, the strongest person always wins in the end. Like those pathetic scrawny dogs who got whipped by the mastiff that took their bone. I thought that was dumb of them—they must have known they never stood a chance. Besides, hearing that we'd been mentioned on the radio, that brought everything from the day before back to me in a rush. And I was beginning to miss Joséphine and my friends. How long would it be before I saw them again? I was so down in the dumps that I would have drunk anything and accepted any offer. It's tiring, loneliness, and not everyone is born with the mettle for resistance. Mariéla had heard like me, without seeming too affected by the news. She almost seemed happy, which infuriated me. It was all her fault. Without knowing what I thought, she made me promise something. When they capture us, promise me not to tell them anything. We don't have to explain. No one explained the beginning to us, everything that happened before. Why should we try to share the end with them? What's ours stays ours. Our share of bitterness and silence. And dreams, too. Promise me to tell them nothing. I promised. She didn't believe me. It wasn't like the day before anymore. We were walking quite close to one another without being completely together. Lots of things separated us. Her strength. My weakness. When the crowd caught us, they took us to the police station, and a bunch of detectives questioned us. We were an item of interest. Mariéla kept her word, of course. She said nothing, and they held that against her. Me, I talked, because like Joséphine, I don't know how to live alone. They took my weak point for my best side. They said that confessing is already a sign of remorse. I don't feel truly guilty. Later, when they separated us for real, each of us locked away in a building with others of our age and sex, I thought over what Mariéla said about the beginning. The beginning, that's our life. Our life killed Corazón. Our lousy life, so far from hope, and so close to death. Those aren't my words. I don't speak the language of thinkers. It was Rosemond who said that. He's first in his class and reads books by poets.

As his name suggests, Stammering Jhonny isn't a talker. Words have a habit of lingering in his throat. If it's something important and people can't wait, someone else often finishes his sentences. Nothing like Rosemond, who talks pretty as a picture and got offered a district scholarship to a school in the nicer neighborhoods. But friends aren't made out of words. The second day was Saturday. On Saturday, Fat Mayard takes food to his cousin Rodrigue, who lives in the penitentiary. Soon it'll be three years for this go-round; Rodrigue is on his fourth stay in the big yellow house on the Rue de l'Enterrement. Burial Street . . . And despite the steps taken by the shady lawyer contacted by his family, there's no reason to think Rodrigue will be getting out. Theft is his passion. During his time outside, he spends all his ill-gotten gains on amassing an impressive collection of gangster films. One can cherish a passion, however, without having any gift for it. Every time Rodrigue tries a little burglary in the finer parts of town, he manages to get himself pinched by security guards. The real criminal elements in the city look down on him. At his last arraignment the judge said there was no point in having a trial. Since then Cousin Rodrigue has been living in the penitentiary, and the unlicensed lawyer has not yet been able to meet with him. Fat Mayard basks in reflected glory. Not many of our locals have any dealings with the State. For good or ill. The State is far away. Its existence doesn't affect us, and it remembers us only when forced to by some misfortune. All contact with anything outside our neighborhood is an honor, a boost to prestige. Like us with Mam Yvonne. The Mayard family is very proud to be in conflict with the State, and they show off their mastery of a few rudiments of the lovely language of the law. Even Fat Mayard, whose one real talent consists in feeling up girls, trots out some high-class words for us every now and then: technicality, recidivist. Like all words we don't know, these sound to us rather like insults, or the eternal verities of a superior world. A little like proverbs above and beyond the usual ones, proverbs only for people in the know. The second day was Saturday. Fat Mayard was going to take the weekly food package to his "recidivist" cousin. I was sure that Stammering Jhonny and maybe Marcel would offer to go with him. We hadn't agreed to meet. Jhonny and I, we were like that. We were so often together that each one sort of became the other and guessed his intentions without us having to waste our time talking it over. Our paths knew how to cross without any communication between us. One time we felt like making kites. It was just an idea . . . We hadn't decided anything. I went to collect scrap materials from the trash heap behind the furniture factory. I met Jhonny on the foul-smelling path we kids use as a shortcut. He'd had the same idea, and we went there together. Without exchanging a single word. Jhonny and I, we've always had a kind of friendship without words. The second day was Saturday. I told Mariéla that we had to go over by the penitentiary. I spoke confidently, and she followed me without saying anything. For once, I was taking the lead. We stopped a few yards from the big prison, in front of the delivery entrance of the State Press. Employees were bringing out enormous bundles and throwing them pell-mell into the trunks of a line of government vehicles. Mariéla started to explain to me that this was the latest edition of the *Official Gazette*, which publishes the laws of the Republic and the decisions of the government. I was still mad at her. I didn't want to listen to her. It's the first time that I hated her. My eyes were telling her: this is all your fault. I needed to soak myself in hatred, to have a real tantrum. Mariéla was the only person available. I was close to pitching a fit. That can happen when I'm feeling bad. Corazón used to grab me and immobilize me. He would carry me outside and plunge my face into a basin to calm me down. Fits of nerves, they're the weakling's anger. If you have something to say, face up to it and say it straight out. I wanted to say it straight out to Mariéla. She was watching the deliverymen hoisting the bundles onto their shoulders and letting them drop into the car trunks without taking the trouble to arrange them neatly. The impatient drivers were letting their motors run. When a car was loaded, it took off at an insane speed with its horn blaring or siren wailing, clearing a path through the line of visiting relatives waiting before the main entrance of the penitentiary. There were weeping mothers and wives. And distant relatives, old folks and children who hung their heads or looked off in another direction. They were ashamed to be there and wore apologetic expressions, as if they weren't actually there, really, they'd just been roped into visiting because the prisoner didn't have any other family, or they'd been compelled to stand in for some-one who couldn't come, a mother, a spouse, or a brother who did love the cretin who'd gotten himself locked up. The prison police searched the visitors before let-ting them enter: their pockets, bags, baskets of provi-sions. They even opened the cigarette cartons and boxes of new shoes, presents for businessmen and the children of good families. And in the crowd, Fat Mayard's voice, Fat Mayard's hands lifting up the pot lid: Rodrigue; pumpkin soup; recidivists' section. He passed inspection and vanished into the penitentiary courtyard. Alone. No sign of Jhonny. When we'd com-municated without needing to arrange to meet, I had not yet killed anyone. Each of us thought he knew how far the other would go. Maybe holding Corazón's feet while Mariéla kept hitting him with the wrench had put me in a different category. A kind of upper level or minefield where timid Jhonny would never dare join me. Poor Jhonny. He had never done any-thing serious in his life. It's a far cry from scattering lizards through the Mayard's small house so as to frighten a crazy old lady—who was already afraid on principle of water, the sky, cotton seeds, and anything, really—to helping your sister shatter your father's skull with a lug wrench. Jhonny would not be coming. Loneliness isn't funny. I was angry at Mariéla, Corazón, Jhonny, Joséphine, all of them. Especially Mariéla. I kicked one of the newspaper bundles; the delivery-man couldn't have cared less. I left without telling Mariéla what my intentions were or asking about hers. She followed me, letting me set the pace. It had been my idea, about my friend. And the disappoint-ment was mine as well. I stopped at the Place Carl Brouard. A little nothing of a square. Nothing like the Champ-de-Mars. On the Place Carl Brouard, there is: nothing. On that day, anyway, there was nothing and no one. Only a few brave birds had flown over the stores downtown, the nauseating penitentiary court-yard, and the plastic utensils, second-hand clothing, and American shoes sold in stalls set up beneath the arcades of hardware stores and law offices to come land heavily on some stunted bushes. A few sick and dirty old birds awaiting sundown in the little square with its parched dirt, broken benches, cracked flower pots, pebbles where there should have been grass, dry soil where there should have been blossoms, and a wrought-iron gate as rusty as the bars of the prison's main entrance. The inscription beneath the bust pointed out that Carl Brouard had been a great poet. I think poets can go to hell. This one couldn't even manage to get his name on a pretty square. The Place Carl Brouard is as filthy as a prison courtyard or the alleys in our slum. Withered laurel bushes grow there, more shriveled than a little old lady. The Place Carl

Brouard isn't a proper square. Or even a proper place. And this life, it isn't a life. Nothing is nothing. Everything is everything. Emptiness. Fullness. Waiting, expectation, and the fear of waiting and expectation. All the opposites at once. The thousand ways of seeing death. The coughing fit. And the mental one, too, arriving at the same time. And jumbled thoughts I can't even remember. And shouts. And me wanting to bash my head against the base of the statue. To clear the noise from my brain. To stock up with both calm and violence. Mariéla tried to approach me. So I told her, first with my eyes, then with my mouth, then with my whole body: this is all your fault, while every noise in the world was hammering at my temples. The sound of the wrench cracking bone. And thousands of voices bursting in my brain. The voice of Corazón, who would never speak again. The preacher's hoarse voice. Joséphine's voice, hidden to speak all the better from within. And Stammering Jhonny stammering, breaking off our friendship. Mam Yvonne changing her promises to reproaches. All the voices in the city reciting their proverbs, and the music of the marching bands that crisscross the shantytown during the month of Lent, and the condemned voices in the penitentiary howling Welcome, and the tears of the weeping women who came to help Joséphine mourn. All those voices. And images. Photos. Corazón falling down. Mariéla with the wrench. Joséphine weeping, praying. Me clinging to Corazón's feet, wanting him to fall. Corazón, fallen, his skull split open. The wrench lying by the body. Me trying to get him up again. And Mariéla's mocking laughter. Death isn't a friend with whom you can play tag. When death gets a grip on you, it never lets go. Jhonny turning his back on me. Marcel, Rosemond. All of them. Corazón falling again and Mariéla still with the wrench. Joséphine praying-crying. And the inside of the penitentiary, looking familiar, even though I'd never been there. And Fat Mayard serving me some soup—You, you're worse than a recidivist. And Corazón falling yet again. Dead. And Corazón, come back to life. A bigger liar than ever. Corazón, looking good, in great shape, whirling Mariéla around like a top, helping me fly my kite. Corazón, back to his old self, throwing Joséphine into the back of the room and giving me a little kick in passing to remind me that he hadn't forgotten how much trouble I'd caused him when I had malaria. And all these images and sounds packing into my head like a migraine welling up from my feet, pausing in my throat before invading my brain. And the heat I feel surging through me, and the coughing, a racking cough, impossible to stop, like during my bouts of malaria. And me looking at myself as if I weren't me, me watching myself run, listening to myself screaming It's all your fault. And Mariéla running after me. Mariéla in despair. Perfect Mariéla. Spit it out, as much as you want, because you're all I've got. Cry, yell as much as you want. Bite, if that'll help you to live, because you're all I've got. We have only each other and what's left of our money. Mariéla who doesn't sulk, who loves me in spite of my insults. Mariéla who also hears the racket jammed into my head. She tries to find the words that would silence all that noise. Mariéla, my last refuge, my doomed sister who despairs at the wall of noise that separates us in my head. And Mariéla, alive, who doesn't give up. It's your fault, all of it, and I spit in her face. And I bang my head on the base of the poet's statue. And Mariéla doesn't even bother to protect herself from my spit. Taking me in her arms, because there is no one else to do that. Holding me close. Against her breasts, the breasts of the young woman who offered me my first dance. Against the young woman's breasts that the street mechanic by the railroad tracks touched with his eyes, making me see what he saw, hope for what he hoped for. Against the breasts of the young woman who's in deep shit with me. Against her young woman's breasts that have suddenly grown older, because the more I howl, the more she tries to find the right words, the more I become a weak little child, the more she feels she must be strong enough to become my father, my mother, the sole tenderness of my life. And her peace becomes my peace. My pain and sorrow become hers. I don't hear what she's saying. I can't understand what her words mean. I cling only to their music. Her song gradually beats back the noises and images killing my head. Her voice is as gentle as a happiness that would last for all time. Even when we both know that it's a song of farewell. The future belongs to that strange and impersonal thing called the law. To the law and to rumor. Mariéla's music is sweet and her voice protects us. In her voice there is no past and no future. We are at peace for a while, without memory or fear. We have not yet killed anyone, and nothing will separate us. And I go to sleep. Only this song exists, a song I love as if it were a cradle. Until Marcel and Stammering Jhonny, emerging from the other world, come toward us and stop in front of the statue. As if they had come there just to read the inscription. Marcel was the one who spoke. They didn't have much time. They had shaken off Fat Mayard and followed us from our observation post at the State Press. Marcel was honest about it. He didn't hide the fact that it was Jhonny's idea. The whole time he was talking, Jhonny and I were looking at each other, and our eyes were saying that we were seeing one another for perhaps the last time, on that pathetic square no one ever visited. Except for the birds. Birds that were so dirty, so skinny, such poor excuses for birds that no one would want to hang a dream on them or consider them fair game.

After you left, the mailman went inside the house. He saw Corazón's body and Joséphine asleep on the bed. He thought they were both dead, and while he was shouting bloody murder, he looked around to see if there was a bottle hidden somewhere, to buck up his courage. At the first cry, folks dropped what they were doing and ran toward the uproar. The house filled up in no time. Rumor had it you'd killed your parents. Not wanting to be left out, the mailman insisted on being counted among the victims. You had almost killed him, too. We were among the first to arrive, and we didn't think Joséphine was completely dead yet. Everybody was calling you murderers. The blood on the wrench and the floor was proof enough. The crowd sided with the mailman: innocent people don't run away after breaking everything like dements. The mailman had arrived early, because he enjoyed having a little glass with Corazón, even though it was against regulations. We would talk about boxing. Such a good-looking man. A little violent, true, but you can't choose your temperament, and he didn't deserve to end up like this. It was in the mailman's interest to appear shaken by his discovery: people expecting letters were pissed off at him for pitching the mailbag into the pond. I did not pitch it! Something or someone hit me hard, I had to struggle not to pass out. I don't know which of the kids did it or what the weapon was, a stone or an iron bar. The pain still curdles my guts. What a pity, such a good-looking man. And folks did agree that Corazón was quite handsome. I have to say that we kids did actually envy you a bit for having such a well-built father. We never dared admit that, for fear ours would find out. People kept coming. The place was getting crowded. Jhonny and me, we went up on the roof of the furniture factory so we could follow what was happening without being disturbed. We missed the moment when they realized that Joséphine wasn't dead. The most eager onlookers wanted to know in which direction you'd taken off; others quickly told them that, from the first outcry, groups had formed to set off looking for you. Fat Mayard had sort of let them know where you were heading. The hunters came back empty-handed. We watched all the comings and goings in the house from the factory roof. No one dared touch the body. Now that Joséphine was alive, some women tried to wake her up, but she decided to stay asleep. Other women kept at it and forced her eyes open. As for the men, they had a big debate about what they should do. The more educated ones suggested calling the police, but since they never come when they're called, the others said it wasn't worth it. That's when Joséphine agreed to wake up and saw Corazón's body and the whole neighborhood arguing and milling around in her house. She didn't cry out; her lips were moving, but without making a sound. She didn't weep, either. The women she prays with offered comfort by reminding her that God is with us even in the most difficult hours. Joéphine was alive, but not much. Not really different from the usual Joséphine, more like the one when she's fasting or on retreat, except that her face was more collapsed, and her eyes a bit emptier, as if she were traveling far away and didn't plan on coming back. Reporters began to arrive. We hadn't expected them. A real parade. They made their way timidly, getting lost among the alleys. Homing in on all the noise. The owner of the furniture factory had telephoned them. You can't say that he lives in the slum or considers himself one of us. But he did take the trouble to send an employee to check things out when he heard the first outcry. And he did allow his workers to take a break and go join the crowd. He also phoned the morgue of the university hospital for an ambulance. Then the news media. And the police. The reporters arrived first. Must be that all the radio stations, the important ones along with those nobody listens to, were seriously out of news. Since the alleys are narrow, these folks showed their press cards to avoid being jostled and bothered. First came the radio people, with their notebooks and tape recorders. Egged on by his family, Fat Mayard blocked the way, standing in the middle of the alley that leads to your house. So you couldn't avoid him. He was the last one to have seen you and he described the clothes you were wearing. But since he talks as much as he eats and he'd switched over to the injustice of Rodrigue condemned to live in the penitentiary without ever having a trial, his story took forever, which irritated people. Grown-ups who hadn't seen anything also wanted to weigh in on the matter, so they shouted down the family, who gave in, outnumbered. And every person in the neighborhood who had something to say was able to give an opinion about your behavior and character. The reporters made their way through the throng to the house. They especially wanted to interview Joséphine, and a few walked right over the blood and broken glass. Joséphine was as deaf and dumb as a picture, but well protected anyway, by a whole army of mourners. Whenever anyone asked her a question, one of the women replied for her. Then the television crews arrived. We heard the noise coming up behind us. A 4x4 with a powerful engine, the mobile unit that covers international sports events and ceremonies at the Palais National or the Parlement. The driver got out, grumbling that there was no fucking way to get up those alleys. The car would break down. The crew chief went to ask the factory owner for permission to park the vehicle in front of his business. And the owner said that normally he didn't permit that. The gangs from the slums trashed any cars left there, and then the victims would get angry at him, as though it were his fault. When circumstances were beyond his control, however, well . . . The cameramen filmed the facade of his business to thank him, then continued on foot up the path with the help of a guide, and when the onlookers caught sight of them, they flocked around the cameras. The radio reporters put away their notebooks and tape recorders, saying that they'd gathered enough information for their listeners, but you could tell they were annoyed at being considered second-class. Then we heard a police siren. People instinctively scattered: with the forces of order, you never know what can happen. They arrive for a specific reason and then discover something else to mess with. Most of the crowd preferred to go on home. Especially the youngsters. There were three policemen: two uniformed officers and their boss, a plainclothes detective. Actually, this wasn't the unit the police station had sent after the furniture factory owner called. That unit never arrived. This was a passing patrol that had heard the commotion and come to investigate. Still, they handled things well, clearing away onlookers and making the mourners around Joséphine pipe down. They questioned the mailman and Fat Mayard. They asked if you had any close friends who might know if you'd planned everything ahead of time and where you might have gone. There are always some people who simply can't keep quiet, and they fingered Stammering Jhonny. But he'd need the livelong day to answer all your questions, better just forget it. Jhonny and I, we lay down on the roof so's we could see without being seen. People didn't much want to talk to the police, who also asked whether the dead man had any family. Yes, a mother living abroad. Whether the victim's wife was able to give evidence. No, wept the weeping women. Whether the boy and girl had committed any previous acts of violence against any of their neighbors. No, we can't begin to imagine why . . . Whether the girl had a boy-friend. No one wanted to tackle that question. People did say, just to say something, that the girl was very secretive, tougher than the boy, but a mite too inde-pendent. Pulling a cell phone from his pocket, the plainclothesman went off into a corner to speak with-out interference. His conversation over, he pocketed the phone again and announced the arrival of an ambulance and a justice of the peace, who never did show up, and the ambulance personnel decided not to wait for him. Speaking of the ambulance, it's lucky that the police phoned for one, because the one the factory owner arranged for arrived late that night, after everyone had gone to bed. I'm telling you all this bluntly, since we don't have a lot of time. The ambu-lance attendants had trouble lifting the body. He was so heavy that they needed help hoisting him onto the stretcher. Getting him out of there took a long time. It was a pathetic procession. The body kept getting stuck in the allies. With more help from some strong guys, they got the body down crosswise, by turning it on its side. Sorry, Mariéla: Joséphine came back to earth and she said it's Mariéla, it's not Colin, it's Mariéla. And she went back off somewhere to live with the Lord. At first, the policemen weren't very nice with her. They wanted to question her at all costs. But a lady showed up and introduced herself to the head policeman as a representative from the Women's Action League. And the policeman behaved quite politely with everyone. With his approval, the lady had all the men and the women mourners leave the house. Mam Nénette refused to abandon Joséphine.

I've been her prayer partner the whole fifteen years I've lived in this neighborhood. They let her stay. After a few minutes, the lady from the league went outside. She called over the television technicians busy collecting their cables and loading up their cameras. She said that the league was going to look after the victim, who would soon be able to issue a statement. At first no one understood what she was talking about: Corazón was dead and on his way to the morgue. The lady explained that Joséphine was a victim, too. Victimized by the violence of a husband who runs on alcohol. Now on her own and in charge of two disturbed children: a girl in the throes of adolescence and a sickly boy who had always suffered from severe health problems. We didn't understand all the images in the lady's speech. One thing was certain, at least: she was used to speaking in public. When she was finished, she went inside the house to look for Joséphine. The plainclothes policeman gave a short interview. He spoke of manslaughter, a criminal investigation, and the mission of the police: to conduct a search for you. Everyone was waiting for Joséphine. The reporters were growing impatient, because it was getting dark. Finally Joséphine appeared, supported by Mam Nénette and the lady from the league. The journalists rushed over to her, while the police lined up to cordon off the little group of diehards intent on staying until the end. Joséphine was wearing a clean dress and she had washed her face. She said, Mariéla, I know that it's . . . The league lady tapped her lightly on the arm, and she started over. I loved my husband, and he loved me. Mariéla, I know that it's . . . No.

Mariéla, please come home. You have to bring back Colin. I didn't see a thing, I was sleeping. The lady has promised to help me, to help you. Mariéla, I know that . . . Everybody was disappointed because Joséphine hadn't said anything about the scene of the crime. Only the league lady was pleased, and she wanted to address the cameras again. The reporters explained that night had fallen and no one could see a thing anymore. Plus if they didn't get back to the studio right away with their visuals and interviews, the incident wouldn't make the evening news. The lady didn't want to wait for the next day. She asked the policemen to take Joséphine and her in their car. Joséphine didn't want to leave without Mam Nénette, and the lady said Fine. They trooped off to the police car, the men in front, the ladies behind. The six of them got inside in the same order: men in front, ladies behind. It was over. All that was left was the commentary, the chitchat, and the proverbs that would help talk the night away. Jhonny and me, we climbed down off the factory roof. We didn't want to go home because our families would still be chewing over what had happened, and we wondered where you were going to sleep. Finally Jhonny said that we really did have to go home. And promised, on his stammering honor, that we'll both see you two soon. Given that tomorrow was Saturday and that Colin would come up with the idea of hanging around the penitentiary.

It was time for them to go home. They had reached their limit of acceptable lateness and were afraid of the questions they might be asked. I wanted them to believe that we hadn't done it on purpose and that the misfortune had happened all by itself. Them I could talk to, without breaking my promise to Mariéla. It isn't good for your friends to have a bad impression of you when you're about to be separated. I wanted them to believe me. To accept the words I had for them. An accident, not a real crime. Neither a lie nor a truth. Just the appropriate words to preserve our friendship. As for them, they didn't make a big deal out of it, preferring to act as if the truth didn't exist or weren't at all important. They went off whistling, without making the slightest comment. After they left we didn't linger around the Place Carl Brouard. We walked at random for a while and found ourselves in the student quarter. Future politicians were arguing in the law school courtyard. Sitting on the ground-floor window sills at the engineering school, snappy dressers were rating girls and talking soccer. The medical students were distinguished by their white coats and a different kind of elegance: they seemed to walk on tiptoe, barely touching the ground so as not to hurt themselves on it. White doesn't go well with dead leaves, fruit peels, scribbled-over paper litter, and a thousand greasy fingerprints on the walls. When I had my malaria, I had an appointment once a week at the pediatric clinic. With a young doctor who smiled constantly and spoke softly. He offered me candies. As the weeks went by, I came to consider him my friend. He asked me about my life, my family, my schoolwork. My father did some boxing in the Dominican Republic. Now he works in a garage. My mother takes care of the house, she doesn't go out much and wants to live very close to God. For school, I only go when we have the money. It's my sister who takes care of me. Without knowing her, he appreciated Mariéla and predicted that she would make an excellent nurse, because my health was improving. I didn't see Mariéla spending her life in sickrooms. With a white cap and gloves. Mariéla, she's the open air. The doctor made a big difference in my life. It was good to be sick. I was so proud of having this friend outside our neighborhood. It was a change. He talked to me about his profession, and I learned a lot from him. One day, feeling better, I went to see him without consulting the official appointment slip. He was working. Still smiling, as usual. I waited until the room began to empty out, and I tried to talk to him about asthma and typhoid. In our slum, as soon as a child has trouble breathing or no longer recognizes family members, people say Here we go, it's asthma or else typhoid. The doctor replied that I was cured and that he had a lot of work. And he offered a candy to a little girl in tears on her first visit to the pediatric clinic. I was so stupid. That doctor, I didn't even know his name. I'm not mad at him. It's not really heaven to spend your time grinning like a gaga at hordes of sick kids. I hope that Joséphine hasn't made the same mistake with the league lady. Today she's living with the lady, but the friendship of rich people, it's something that doesn't always last. I love the student quarter. Voices there aren't sad. I'm only sorry that I didn't get to visit the classroom in the music school where they teach the guitar. I didn't understand the theme of the painted mural that covers the facade, it doesn't look like anything I could recognize. It's true that you could say the same thing about life, sometimes. In the street, the newspaper and snow cone vendors competed for the students' custom. Mariéla asked me for a five-gourde piece and bought a newspaper. We went off to sit on a low wall in front of the faculty of science. Mariéla disappeared behind her paper. Her legs were spread out from the way she was sitting. Her dress was hiked up to her thighs. Across from us, a student in a white coat was trying to see more. His eyes were reading below the newspaper. Without realizing it, Mariéla was spreading her legs even more. The whole time she was reading the paper, I was watching a street photographer who specialized in identification pictures. He had set up his equipment in the carcass of a minibus. Students would go inside and sit on the stool. The photographer would arrange the students' collars, position their faces at the right angle, pull the curtain, and take the picture. The medical students had to take off their white coats, and sitting there in their ordinary clothes, they finally looked like everyone else. The ID photos are for passports and requests for visas. Mam Yvonne had suggested that we have some pictures taken. We didn't always have enough to eat, but she wanted every member of the family to have a separate passport. To make us that much more ready to leave. There are lots of passports hidden under the mattresses of our shantytown. Little blue books with blank pages. Waiting. The newspaper talked about that. Mariéla had read enough. She had looked up and noticed where the student was looking. She handed me the paper; now the student had a full view of her. Without changing her posture, she smiled at him. Their game irritated me. I can't say that I was jealous, because I haven't the right. She smiled at me, too, as if giving me permission to look. Telling me that I could join the game. But I didn't dare. I chose the newspaper article. About our desire to travel. About Corazón, who had only lasted halfway through the first round against El Negro. About the pages missing from Corazón's life after that boxing match, the years that no one knew anything about. About his return one evening. Ten years too late. About his father who threw him out, because You're twenty-five years old, it's time to grow up. About Joséphine, an orphanage girl, whom the nuns taught to obey orders. Joséphine, whom he'd brought into the slum. A husband who treats you like dirt, that's better than a gaggle of good sisters acting as your father and mother. About us.

Who hadn't forgiven Corazón for preventing us from enjoying the inheritance from Mam Yvonne. About us, who were now a national problem. About Mam Yvonne, whom the journalists hadn't managed to contact by phone. About Mam Yvonne, who would grow old alone in Florida. About the lady from the Women's Action League asking for donations to support Joséphine. The article was too long, with small print. I read only part of it. Mariéla had kept the paper for half an hour. Time enough for the daylight to begin dwindling. Although it was not yet evening, reading wasn't easy. Students were leaving their schools. The med students folded up their white coats and put them in their bags. Groups were forming as the students headed off in different directions. We happened to follow the largest group, which set out for the stadium, where some star foreign players would be out on the field that night. As we walked along, I threw away the newspaper, to have my hands free. Besides, it had terrified me to see our names on the first page. I remember. There was an article inside the paper even longer than the one about us in "Current Events," a piece devoted to a city in the south that was celebrating a Sea Festival. There were photos, and anyone interested was invited to the festival. I don't know which article Mariéla spent so much time on. I didn't ask her. The next day, right when they caught us, when we'd lost sight of each other, carried off by separate halves of a crowd hungry for justice, she yelled, Little brother, we'll meet up in Pestel. Which is, I'm pretty sure, the name of that city in the newspaper.

There were as many people outside the stadium as there were inside it. The security guards were refusing entry to the unlucky guys who had bought fake tickets from scam artists. The disappointed fans weren't leaving, they were hanging around to look for the crooks. Most people hadn't bought tickets. They had just enough money to treat themselves to something to drink, a beer, an accra-fritter, or a bite of pork. To follow the match, they had brought along dozens of transistor radios tuned to the government station. I was afraid of meeting someone who knew us in that crowd. An ugly surprise, like Romulus showing up on the Champ-de-Mars. With his discipline and order. Especially since everyone in the city must have heard about us. I looked for a dark corner off somewhere. Mariéla didn't share my uneasiness. Instead, she seemed irritated. Annoyed by my presence. On the way to the stadium, some students had come up to her, including the one she had smiled at. I didn't trust him. Mariéla was nervous, looking for someone in the throng, constantly asking what time it was. As if she were afraid of missing an appointment. Finally, unable to stay in one place anymore, she told me she had something to do, that I could wait for her right by the stadium, on the side across from the cemetery. She would be there when the match was over. She left. She turned around to give me one of her smiles. It was a studied smile. Not a real one. Not one like the smiles she flashes me after Corazón has given me a licking. When I'm in pain she smiles at me, to share the blows. Or she lets her arm lie on my side of the mattress. And I fall asleep content, clinging to my branch. The second evening, she took off. She was going to return, of course. But she had chosen something that wasn't me. Something, or someone. The whole time we were together, maybe she was always alone. I hadn't thought of that . . . Her leaving made us even. At the risk of being spotted by one of our neighbors from the slum, I left my corner. I walked through all the noise. The radios were announcing the lineup of each team; the crowd reacted to the names by commenting on the coaches' decisions. We could hear the real spectators' cries of impatience from inside the stadium. And then, everything came to a halt. For the national anthem. That's the only poem I know by heart. My teacher had insisted on that. Every honest citizen venerates the flag and knows the words to the national anthem. I can recite the words; as for that other business, I don't know much. Except for what Mam Yvonne had to say about it. That once upon a time the flag meant something for the government, the citizenry, our young people. But nowadays, it doesn't mean anything. It's just a faded piece of cloth fought over by dogs. Then everyone came back to life again. The people outside followed the match as if they were inside, cheering at a dribble or a good save by the goalie. At first that seemed silly to me. To act as if they could see the action. When our team scored, the spectators outside the stadium shouted along with those inside. I let myself get caught up in the game, and like everyone else, I saw that the goal was a beauty, and that the referee had made a mistake in not allowing the second goal. And then, when the other team evened the score, I saw that our defense had botched the play, that our captain was limping, and that our coach was waiting too long to replace him. I saw those things without seeing them. I told one of the detectives that I was at the stadium and that I wasn't there. He thought I was talking nonsense. He said I was just a smart aleck pretending to be mentally ill. And yet, it was the truth. I was there and I wasn't. I think that I could describe the stands if I were asked about their shape and colors. I was there for the first half. Then Mariéla's absence became unbearable. And from then on I could think of nothing but her. During half-time, some of the fans who'd been scammed spotted one of the crooks, who made the mistake of falling into their hands with his pockets full of counterfeit tickets. His victims tore up his clothes and stuffed tickets into his mouth. Saved by the start of the second half, he took off like a shot, leaving behind the shreds of his shirt and a few drops of blood. I didn't follow the second half. I thought that Mariéla and I might suffer the same fate. I went to wait for her at the side entrance facing the cemetery. I sat down on the ground, where I was in the way. A security guard asked me to move. I scooted a little farther off on my bum. Echoes of the match reached me every now and then. I saw Mariéla's back, a footbridge, people around me, thousands of them, and I still saw Mariéla's back, still turned, as if her face had become something forbidden; I heard voices shouting at me to move aside a little, I felt legs brushing against me and I saw Mariéla's back again, just her back, naked, moving away, and I called, but she didn't hear me, and I called her so she would turn around and remember me, and one of the voices around me demanded that I stop screaming. A foot kicked me. Right in the face. After that everything disappeared. Mariéla, the voices. When I woke up, there wasn't a living soul besides the dead in the cemetery. Corazón's new world. In the slum folks say the dead have another life there and spend their time commenting on ours. The dead talked to me about the reality of the world that comes before theirs. The dead told me that Mariéla would never come back. The time for our rendezvous was long gone. Just one against all of them—no living person can fight the dead. Corazón spoke for them. He had become their leader. And he spoke like a living man. He comes to see me when I'm alone. Even now. It's because I don't want to hear him that I'm telling this story. Whether there's anyone to listen to it . . . or whether there's only me. He comes whenever he can. To talk to me about boxing. And to tell me why he fixed things so that no one would understand his plans or his decisions. There is only one key that opens the gates of wisdom:

There's no one for you but yourself. Mariéla had gone. I still had the night and the song of the cemetery. I was almost resigned to this when Mariéla showed up. A brand-new Mariéla, happy and unhappy. She told me a little hesitantly that we had enough to pay for a room in a local main-street hotel, one of those seedy places with shabby facades frequented by whores and drug addicts. It was a lot better than the cemetery. I wanted to know where she'd gotten the money. That student gave it to me. Why? What do you care? Why are you asking me that? Because I was right to be suspicious of that student. Because you went off to join him. Because of all the reasons I didn't give. So what. He's gone. There's just the two of us. There was just the two of us. Walking toward the main street. Leaving the cemetery, the empty stadium, and the wrong side of the night behind us. Mariéla picked out the hotel. They were all the same except for their names. She chose My Lucky Star. The manager didn't ask any questions. The room was on the second floor. Not expensive. Not expensive enough to have running water and a fan. We moved closer together in the dimly lit hall. The door was open. A bed. Dirty sheets. A warped floor. And cockroaches. A wash basin. Filth like ours. As if we had paid to sleep at home. As if we were at home even while we were somewhere else. In our own little slum. A lonely little slum that goes up and down the streets like the sweeper boy in the nursery rhyme. In the shit. And on a star.

The poor follow in the footsteps of the poor: all we knew were the flat places where a crowd makes the landscape. Chance and necessity always lead us to the same spots. In our part of the city. In slums like ours. After all, it's not so bad. It's easier to bear your life when it's the only one you know. Once a year, Joséphine would go pray at Saint-Charles. I would follow her all the way to Carrefour, a poor neighborhood so full of people that their movement hides everything: the houses, the sea . . . In Carrefour, aside from the people, all you can see is the sun that lives alone up there like some sort of god without any family. Carrefour, it's like where we live. Only bigger. A slum as big as a country. To survive, we preferred to believe that the whole world was like ours. With lots of Joséphines. With Corazóns. With a single season, always bad. Mam Yvonne's letters would arrive full of advice and news of electronic marvels. Mariéla would read them. Joséphine had learned to read at the good sisters' orphanage, in that distant past she never mentions. For a long time she never used her reading, except for the Bible, and she's gotten rusty at it. We used to wait for Corazón to leave for the garage. Off he'd go, always in a hurry, with his toolbox and his lies. Mariéla would read the letters out loud, going over the most important passages twice. We felt that Mam Yvonne was exaggerating, that she was showing us the good aspects of her trip on purpose to encourage us to follow her. If only Colin would . . . Corazón, all he wanted was our rotten shack, his boxing, his overalls. And the presence of Joséphine. Not even her body. Just her presence. He used to tell her Don't bother closing the curtain, I don't feel like it, you can do it with your God. Corazón sometimes said hard words. Or else he told lies. To himself, to others. Or he spoke to hurt Joséphine. Him, he'd crossed a border, to see things, and people. But he had returned. He hadn't brought back a woman from over there, he had married an orphanage girl who was sad by nature. To hear Corazón talk, it was the same thing everywhere. But on the third day, we took a long trip. To the land of tourists. To get an idea, to see for ourselves. One thing I learned: no one can serve as an example. No one is right and no one is wrong. It's life that's wrong. On the third day, we went up the mountain. The one you can see from our neighborhood when the sky is clear. Without being sure that it really does exist. Without being sure that you have any right to it. That you could climb there and run through the greenery. Ambroise went there once. With his mother, who worked as a cleaning woman in a villa. He talked about it as if it were a foreign land. The third day, that was the first time we'd ever gone to the mountain. In the truck, we studied the landscape along the way. The trees. The houses. The satellite dishes on the roofs. The dogs, too. With happy tails. We took thousands of pictures in our heads. For later. Instead of the sea, which we may never get a look at, we'll have the mountain. We had it. And we were comparing the sights. Like real travelers. I liked the slate roofs and the big dogs that don't look so mean. Mariéla—it was as if she had already known. What we were seeing came straight out of the school compositions she'd once written for me. It was a little as if she had done like God, creating a world in her head that suddenly became real because she had imagined it. We paid the fare and got out of the truck. The air was cool, and the sun more gentle than ours. We still had a few coins left. Enough to get back down to the city. From high up, it didn't look threatening. On the contrary, you could imagine the sand mines that tunneled into the mountain's slopes sending it crashing down there one day.[5] Crushing the city with the weight of its flowers. We managed to make out the stadium, the cemetery, the cathedral, and a few other buildings. We tried to find our neighborhood, but we didn't have any landmarks. All slums look alike. We bought some mulberries. We'd never seen this fruit before. The lady told us that they grow only in Kenskoff, where the temperature is cooler than in the rest of the country. Then Mariéla asked her what was the best place for getting a view of the entire city. The question surprised the fruit seller, who realized that we weren't from around there. She pointed to the road sign indicating the direction to Boutilliers. As we started off along the road, she said, The hill is steep, and the guides don't like beggars. As we climbed, we saw big trucks hauling sand for houses under construction. And a mine, a little farther along on our left. Now, that's a job. If Corazón had had a real job, maybe he would still be alive. But Corazón had only one plan, to be a boxer, punch in the faces of a whole bunch of opponents, and be world famous. Even when he'd gotten too old, he was still dreaming about it. And everything that he did didn't really exist. The garage. Us. Joséphine. His lies. The alcohol. The past. His father who had preferred to die so as not to help him live in his dream. Corazón, he lived all alone. And the more time passed, the more alone he was. With a dream in the back of his mind. Matches he was going to fight that had never taken place. That's why he didn't think it necessary to leave the slum. He never lived there. He spent his life in the ring. And Mam Yvonne's house, it was pretty, but it wasn't a boxing ring. A chandelier? That's not worth a championship title. Maybe if we had listened to him, if we had known how to get inside his dream, he would have been happier. The problem is, there's not enough happiness for everyone to give some away. Not in our slum, anyway. In Boutilliers, perhaps there's enough. Rental cars were going by. The passengers were laughing. It's truly a beautiful place. We made it to the top and we walked among foreigners with cameras and big hats. Guides were talking to them with lots of gestures. And the foreigners understood and answered with just as many gestures to show that they were thirsty or would like to sit down. I didn't want to get too close, but they were taking the best spots. Mariéla wanted to see the city. We went to stand next to a couple of tourists. The guide was furious. He explained to the tourists that they had to watch out for little thieves pretending to be beggars. The lady wanted to take a photograph. The man, a hairy guy who smiled at us as though we were babies, showed the lady how to use the camera. Behind them, the guide was shaking his fist at us. Mariéla didn't give a spit. She looked at the city spread out below us. The lady finally figured out the camera and was exclaiming at how beautiful the scenery was. She wanted to photograph everything. The plants. The sky. The fruit. The guide. Us. She asked our permission. The man said he would pay us. That it was their first trip to this part of the world and that they thought the people were very sweet. Mariéla asked how much he would pay, and he gave us a ten-dollar bill. I put it in my pocket. The lady placed us in the position she wanted. Against a tree. She took a first picture that she didn't think was good enough. We had forgotten to smile. She gave us the photo on condition that she could take another one. In the second picture, we smiled like robots. That one she liked. She kept it. The hairy man thanked us. The guide told them that it was time to leave. But they wanted to stay longer, because it was their first trip and everything was so lovely in this part of the world: the trees, the people. Us, with our clothes that were beginning to stink. The guide with his hoarse voice, his yellowed teeth, and his faded, worn-out flowered shirt. In Boutilliers, the air is very cool. They say it's always cool there, whatever the season. My cough had returned. We started back down the hill. Mariéla walked in front of me. I trailed along behind. We knew it was our last holiday. The first one, the last one. A day that didn't fit into the weekly schedule. A day outside of time. Belonging to no family or calendar. We had decided to give ourselves up that evening. To go to the police station closest to our neighborhood. The smartest thing to do would have been to go to the address given to the newspaper by the Women's Action League lady. Mariéla didn't want to involve Joséphine in our problems. Joséphine—she'd hear about it from the police. And she would decide. To visit us or hate us. Joséphine, she doesn't know it yet (she has never liked knowing, just suffering and praying), but she doesn't owe us anything, she's free. No one owes anyone anything. That's how Mariéla was talking, coming down the hill from Boutilliers. My cough was back again. Because of the cool air and the humidity. I felt a little cold. But it's very pleasant to feel so close to the sky. To have all that blue within reach. To run so near the clouds one Sunday morning. The guide spoke up behind my back. The money my client gave you—you've got to share it with me. Mariéla turned around. Instinctively, I put my hand in my pocket to protect the ten dollars. The guide was angry. That's the rule. You have to share. Everybody shares: the drivers, the guides, the thieves, the beggars. You can't come out of nowhere and just go off with money people worked for. Three days I've been driving them all over. First, it was the beach, then the markets, then the handicraft shops, and now here. You have to share. Or I'll take the money from you. He seemed mean, and what he was saying made some sense. But we had promised ourselves a Sunday. An afternoon on the Place des Héros. A moment to ourselves, without anyone putting the seal of a crime or any trouble on our lives. A moment that was free and clear. A sort of time beyond time when we would be creatures without cause or consequence. The ten dollars would be enough for us to become, for a moment, the children of heroes. As if we had been born to be happy. On the square. At the foot of the statues. The guide would never have understood. He had been a guide for fifteen years—And I'm telling you that's the rule! Mariéla asked him if he ever listened to the radio. If he'd happened to listen recently. If he might have heard about the two crazy kids who'd killed their father and were wandering around the city, each armed with a dagger. Us, we don't share. We take. And when people bother us, we kill. The guide knew our story. He backed off. My hand was still in my pocket, holding tight to the ten-dollar bill. But when you're frightened, you see things that exist and things that don't exist. He saw the dagger. And began to scream bloody murder, backing away. But his cries didn't interest the passing cars. He went back up the hill to call for help from his colleagues. And we rushed down the slope. We fought for a seat in a truck heading down to the city. In the truck, I pulled the crumpled bill and the photo from my pocket. It's true that we looked sad in our wrinkled, dirty clothes. But behind us was the tree. And behind the tree, emptiness. It's beautiful, emptiness. Probably because emptiness has neither consciousness nor memory. The truck was speeding along, and the landscape kept getting crummier the closer we got to the city. I thought about Mam Yvonne, who would have been ashamed of us, because we had accepted money from a stranger. Mariéla guessed what I was thinking, though, and said it didn't matter at all. The third day, that was Sunday. And in the shantytown, on Sunday, everyone spruces up. Even the ugliest folks want to look good. Oldsters try to seem young again. Ladies sweep their doorsteps, sprinkling water every which way to lay the dust. Sunday, that's the day when people change their looks and take a rest from their unhappiness. Corazón used to swap his overalls for a sky blue undershirt that set off his physique. Joséphine would suck on her hard candies. Jhonny stuttered less. Even Fat Mayard knew how to turn nice and spend the day without insulting girls. Like true children of the slum, we'd decided to have ourselves a Sunday.

Back in the city, we avoided the foreign exchange offices. A clerk with a good memory for faces might have recognized us. We used to accompany Joséphine when she went to exchange the money Mam Yvonne sent us. Joséphine didn't like to walk in the street alone, never mind speak to a stranger on her own. Mariéla was usually the one who talked. The clerks would comment on her intelligence. Mariéla thanked them and handed the envelope to Joséphine, who was always astonished to see that a simple green bill changed into local currency became a large sum of money. For Joséphine, life is limited to two things: miracles and penance. The envelope was a miracle, and protecting it, a penance. Corazón would get itchy fingers when a little bird told him that Mam Yvonne had written. Mam Yvonne rarely wrote without sending us money. There were always some dollars hidden in her correspondence. About every four letters, Joséphine would suggest to Mariéla that we send her a reply. We'd buy a sheet of white paper and an airmail envelope at old man Eliphète's variety store. Mariéla would write. Joséphine and I would each scrawl our names at the bottom of the letter. Then Joséphine would get back to her housework. Mariéla and I would go off to the main post office. Mariéla would let me choose the stamp. Sometimes the postal clerk was in a hurry or grumpy and wouldn't let me choose. To an employee of the main post office, all stamps must look alike. The subject isn't important—it's only the face value that counts. And the sale. A day at work is just another day at work. To us, anything could become extraordinary. A stamp was a marvel. Or a toad. A helicopter trailing a banner through the sky over the city during an election campaign. A pen. A guitar. A Sunday. We exchanged the bill on the sidewalk, on the corner of John Brown and Martin Luther King streets. The money changer there doesn't ask any questions. He opens his bag and hands you the bills. Without an envelope or a receipt. At three in the afternoon, we had in our pockets enough to have ourselves a Sunday. Each with half. Each with dreams. And the right not to think about a single thing. At that hour, the Place des Héros wasn't crowded yet. Just some boys my age playing soccer, four against four, bare chested, their shirts lying on the grass. I was never a good player. They say there's no better school than the alleys of a slum to develop good dribbling technique: you must make every move in such a small space. Playing soccer in the slum, it's like dancing on a hankie. The other kids aren't bad. Me, I cough and tire easily. I've never belonged to a team. It's as though nature took revenge on Corazón through me. And I remind myself that chance comes in for some of the blame. With his muscles, Corazón deserved better. Chance doesn't dole out the children you're hoping for. It's the same for Mam Yvonne, who'd wanted to be the mother of a lawyer, and Joséphine, who expected a girl like her to help her cry. The lower the sun sank, the livelier the square became. The little soccer players lost their fields to people out for a late-afternoon stroll. Gaming tables were set up, and gamblers gathered around the dealers. Mariéla takes my hand. I don't yet know that it's for the last time. Perhaps she knows. Her hand is firm, like sound advice. As tender as an eternity. Her hand promises me a rendezvous, saying goodbye, forever, till we meet again. And we go together to play roulette. She bets on the sixteen. Why sixteen? Because it's the date of your birthday. Because while she brought you into this world Joséphine wept and prayed. Corazón had gone out into the alley. He didn't want to watch the birth. He was afraid you'd be born a girl like me. Me, I was so small. And you, when you came out of Joséphine's belly you were even smaller than I was. On sixteen, again. But that's the third time we've lost. Doesn't matter. You were tiny as anything, and the midwife told Joséphine that you'd never be very big. And Corazón, who'd come back when they'd told him it was a boy, left again, and we didn't see him for some time. When he finally returned, you were already walking. I hadn't forgotten his face. He showed up one evening, drunk. With his overalls and his toolbox. And Joséphine thanked heaven for its mercy. Me, I took a wrench from the toolbox, to hit him. The wrench was too heavy. I fell down, and that made him laugh. He took me in his arms to whirl me around like a top. And while I was turning, everywhere and nowhere, dizzy with speed, I kept pummeling him with my fists. I was hitting and he was laughing. I couldn't manage to hurt him. He was proud of me. He set me down on the ground and said Too bad you're not a boy. Yes, actually, we do want to bet on the sixteen again, and what the fuck do you care where our money comes from? On the tenth bet, we finally win. Not much. Much less than we've lost. And much more. Because Mariéla, she wanted to show me that she has confidence in my birth. She reminds me of my promise never to explain anything, tell anything, justify, implore. Nothing about the past or these hours that belong to us. I promise once more to live in silence, to make it our territory, where nothing and no one will ever break in. Neither the crime, nor any authority. But Mariéla knows I won't keep my promise. She says if you have to tell—try to make it a beautiful story. It's no harder than a school essay. And we leave the gamblers to gamble. We walk aimlessly. We haven't much time left now. We don't know it yet, and time matters little to us. We watch lovers kissing. Basically, we're almost lovers. Mariéla lets go of my hand. She wants a bike ride. She knows how to ride. I want to follow her. She points the bandstand out to me. The Sunday orchestra is setting up. Go over there. Or you won't be able to see the conductor with his wand. I follow her in spite of her advice. She waits. She pays for a complete ride around the square. She picks out her bike. She gets on it. I see her face smiling, her legs. Her young woman's breasts are steady as she goes, riding slowly forward and looking back to smile at me. One last time. But I don't yet know that it's the last time. The orchestra begins to play. I can't make my way through the crowd to get near the musicians. I would have liked to see the music. Finally, behind a huge guy who sticks out his elbows to get more room for himself, I manage, by craning my neck to one side, between the hip and the elbow, to glimpse a few bits of the conductor. First I see his shoes. But shoes don't say anything. His are clean, that's all they say. Then I see his hands. Writing music in the air. Gently watering the square. His hands that aren't hitting, aren't wounding. His hands that are no longer his hands but the hands of music. I bump into the big guy, who glares at me. I move a bit farther away. Now that I've seen what hands can do, I know one part of Mariéla's secret. You can transform the smallest thing into what it is not. It's with the hands of music that she used to write my compositions. With a single image she kept in her head and that could open everything for her. The hands of the music carry me away. I'm everywhere on my patch of grass. In a different light from the one shed by the lampposts gleaming on the square. In the light of Mariéla who is riding her bike and will never forget the date of my birthday. In the light of Corazón who takes us both in his arms, twirling us like a top. In the light of Joséphine who reminds Corazón that their first love story ended in bloodshed and that they haven't the right to botch the second one. In the light of Stammering Jhonny who one day will run his big kite factory and offer the sky to thousands of children. In all the lights of the world lit on the square. And I look up. I no longer see Jhonny with his kites. I see the statues of heroes who don't hear the music. I'm the only one left who hears the music. I'm the only one left who doesn't see that the roulette players, the concert audience, the ice-cream vendors, the guys renting out bikes, the whole square is running after Mariéla who kicks out, punches, gets away, confronts the crowd, stands up to them, falls, gets up again, says nothing and says Whatever you do don't tell them anything unless you make it a beautiful story. The whole square. Except me. The musicians. And the statues. It's been days or years since that happened. But what does that matter to you? And what does it matter to me? That I've been telling my story since yesterday to the police and the detectives, or since I lost my mind, to people who don't exist. I don't know where it begins. After all, I don't know much about it. Mariéla could explain it to you better, but she says that in flesh and blood, you people will never be worth the trouble. She says that flesh-and-blood people can't go beyond themselves and they miss their truth by a mile. She prefers to imagine you. Me, I've already told you all I can say about it. It must have been noon when we began to run.

1. One gourde is worth 100 centimes, and five gourdes make a *dollar haïtien*.

2. After the capture of Toussaint L'Ouverture, his chief lieutenant, Jean-Jacques Dessalines, led the only successful slave rebellion in history on to victory: on January 1, 1804, he proclaimed the independence of the former French colony of Saint Domingue, which he renamed Haiti. Dessalines became governor-general-for-life and soon thereafter was crowned emperor of Haiti under the name of Jacques I.

Dessalines attempted to revive the nation's devastated sugar-and coffee-based export economy by enforcing a harsh regimen of plantation labor. The black masses, disappointed in their hopes for land reform, and the mulatto elite, fearing for their property and commercial rights, turned against Dessalines. Both Henri Christophe and Alexandre Pétion, his former comrades in arms, backed a conspiracy to overthrow the emperor, who was ambushed and killed at Pont Rouge, a bridge near Port-au-Prince, on October 17, 1806.

A vengeful mob bore Dessalines's mutilated body into Port-au-Prince and dumped it in the dust to be stoned by children and fought over by pigs and dogs. The story goes that a madwoman named Défilée, hearing that the now unrecognizable corpse was that of the emperor, ran to get a coffee sack to carry the pitiful remains to the Inner Cemetery, where she placed the sack on a grave and knelt before it in prayer.

3. In the heart of Port-au-Prince, the Champ-de-Mars is the civic, cultural, and political center of the capital. After the Haitian Revolution, a large park adjacent to the palace

of the French colonial governors became the parade ground of the Haitian army and was soon baptized "the Field of Mars." In 1907 the site was beautified with plantings, paths, fountains, a monument to Jean-Jacques Dessalines, and a bandstand where concerts were given under the auspices of the Palais National, which had replaced the palace of the colonial governors. In 1954 to mark the 150th anniversary of Independence, the Champ-de-Mars was divided into various squares, four of which were dedicated to the Fathers of the Haitian Nation—L'Ouverture, Dessalines, Christophe, and Pétion—whose imposing statues grace the park thereafter known officially as the Place des Héros-de-l'Indépendance.

4. The neighborhood of Bas Peu de Chose (literally, "Lower Not Much"), which lies near the Champ-de-Mars, still boasts some turn-of-the-century houses with lovely "gingerbread" woodwork ornamentation, as well as the most famous mansion in Port-au-Prince: the Villa Sam. Designed by a French architect in 1887 for Démosthène Sam, whose father was President of Haiti at that time, this elegant villa became the Grand Hôtel Oloffson, immortalized in Graham Greene's 1966 novel, *The Comedians*.

5. Southeast of downtown Port-au-Prince lies the well-to-do neighborhood of Pétionville, which begins the ascent of the eastern flank of Le Morne de l'Hôpital, the small mountain of volcanic origin that rises directly to the south of the Haitian capital. The sand quarries of Laboule produce calcium carbonate of great purity, but the immense white gashes they cut into the southern face of the mountain are an ecological nightmare.

Continuing up the morne to the lofty Belvédere de Boutilliers, one may view the Bay of Port-au-Prince and the capital itself to the north, and to the east, on a clear day, lakes, mountains, and even the western border of the Dominican Republic.

Due south of Pétionville is Kenscoff, which enjoys a pleasant climate all year round thanks to its great elevation. Kenscoff is at the center of a rich agricultural region, and the market there is famous for its varied produce.